Ruth Meyer
August 12, 1942

NURSES ARE PEOPLE

BY THE SAME AUTHOR

NURSE IN WHITE
BLOOD OF HER ANCESTORS
MEET THE WARRENS
NORTH SIDE NURSE
GAY PRETENDING
CHRISTMAS GIFT
BROWN HONEY

LUCY AGNES HANCOCK

Nurses Are People

TRIANGLE BOOKS
New York

TRIANGLE BOOKS, 14 West Forty-ninth Street,
New York, N. Y.

PRINTED AND BOUND IN THE UNITED STATES OF AMERICA
BY THE AMERICAN BOOK—STRATFORD PRESS, INC., N. Y. C.

To
Mary Karen Fisher
" All the good fairies attended her
christening and each brought a gift."

NURSES ARE PEOPLE

Chapter 1

DID LONGWORTH SAY ANYTHING ABOUT YOUR BEING OUT last night, Cooper?" Roberta Cameron asked as Cynthia Cooper yawned audibly.

"Say anything! Oh no—not much. Merely mopped the office floor with my reputation so it's hanging in shreds from the broken halo I've worn successfully, lo, these two and more years. Wow! It's a wonder I'm here at all."

Her voice deepened and it was the superintendent of nurses at Weston General Hospital speaking:

"'I am surprised and disappointed, Cooper, gravely disappointed. You are thoroughly aware of the rules forbidding student nurses having any social intercourse whatsoever with the male members of the staff. And yet you deliberately—I repeat—deliberately flaunt your disdain of those rules by attending a dance with one of the internes. I shall see that Doctor Davis is made aware of the regulations governing the staff of this hospital if he doesn't already know them. Another such infringement on your part, Miss Cooper, will be treated much more drastically, I assure you. That is all.' Poor Davis! He's as shy as a fawn, whatever that is. Do you know, girls, sometimes I wonder why I ever came to this hospital in the first place. Are we women—are we human or are we automatons?'"

"Just now I'm terribly, painfully human," groaned Tess Everson. "I'll have to go to the chiropodist again this week. My darned feet drive me crazy."

"Why don't you let——" began Roberta, twirling a rat-tail comb and eyeing the neat rows of curls on the small dark head before her.

"Merrill? No thanks," murmured Tess. "He hurt like hades the one time I went to him. I prefer Mrs. Clark—at least she's gentle and for a while the poor doggies feel heavenly. If it only would last!"

"It's the weather, Everson," Roberta told her. "Change of weather or seasons always plays havoc with feet." She extended a slim white-shod foot for inspection. "See these shoes, girls? Special soles—some sort of composition—built-in supports—warranted to ease the strain of standing. Longworth hasn't spotted them yet; when she does I hope the worst will be over. Who's next? Instead of finishing training here I think I'll open a beauty salon. Thar's gold in them thar heads—if little else." She dodged as Cynthia Cooper caught up a pillow.

"Ye-ah!" jeered Myrtle Andrews, reaching for a hand mirror and inspecting the back of her head. "How much do you make out of this gang? We're a bunch of heels, Bobby. Why do you bother?"

"It's no bother," Roberta insisted. "I like doing it. Anyway, none of us has any money and you all do things for me."

"Such as?" queried Cynthia. "I've offered you every dud in my clothes closet and some of Helen's and you turn up your nose at them. Yes, you do, Cameron, and then last night you simply stampeded me into wearing your newest evening frock. You're a swell kid, Bobby Cameron; but you're something of a nut, too. Lucky for me nothing happened to that dress."

"Don't let my generosity embarrass you, girls," Roberta soothed, sprinkling waving lotion on Tess's heavy chestnut hair. "Most of my clothes are gifts from my sister whose taste is certainly not mine. If Beth would only give me the money the things cost, I could buy what I want. But no, I'm supposed to be a moron where clothes are concerned. She's so darned sweet about sending me the things she feels sure are suitable to my particular type, that I simply can't spoil her pleasure. I'm sorry," she exclaimed as Tess uttered a shrill "Ouch!"

"You should worry," Myrtle said. "You'd look like a million in a sarong. I remember when we were probies and wore those atrocious blue ginghams you were the only one in the entire class who didn't look like some poor, neglected orphan."

"Thanks," Roberta replied dryly. "Do you want a receipt for that?"

"Uh-uh." The other shook her head. "That's gratis."

The girls were loafing in Roberta's room in the nurses' annex. All were on night duty. Cynthia Cooper had cajoled another student into exchanging her free night in order that she might attend a dance in Axton with one of the internes. Roberta couldn't explain just why she continued this practice of finger-waving and setting hair for her fellow students. She had given a finger-wave to her roommate late one stormy afternoon when the girl had a special dinner date and no money. The result was so satisfactory her fame spread throughout the hospital and from then on she was in demand.

"You're lucky to get your four days right now," offered Tess, admiring her shining waves. "March brings measles and flu and pneumonia. It's fool's spring we're having and we're in for a siege, you'll see. Those clouds mean snow, my friends, or I'm no weather prophet."

"You're as bad as Jeremiah," jeered Roberta. "Always making dire predictions that never materialize—that is, almost never. He has dumped me into one or two tough spots."

"Why don't you turn the old jalopy in, Bob?" Tess

asked. "If you wait much longer you'll have to pay the salesman to take it away. Get one of those swanky new convertibles——"

"Using what for money? Uh-uh," she shook her head. "Jeremiah will have to do for a while. Anyway, in spite of his groanings, he takes me where I want to go and brings me back—in his own good time. That's all any car will do. I hope you're wrong about the weather, Tess, because Beth and Will are at the cottage and it's a two hundred mile drive—somewhat less if I take the short cut."

"No short cuts, my child," Cynthia advised. "Stick to the state roads, then even if it storms you are almost sure to get through. But I think winter's over. I saw two robins this morning——"

"Two robins don't make a spring, Cooper," Tess insisted, "and I feel certain this weather's what we coast dwellers call a breeder. The temperature has dropped thirty degrees since seven this morning. After all, it's still March, bear in mind. Better take the train, Cameron——"

"And walk miles? Not me. Jerry will get me there all right. Don't worry about me, and it's still above freezing. What if it does snow a bit? Spring snowstorms never amount to much."

"Don't they though! I remember an April snowstorm that completely paralyzed traffic for a week. However, I see my advice is not wanted. Thanks for the wave, Cameron, and if I don't see you before you leave—have a swell time. A night in a snowbank might not be so bad, at that. At least you'd be quiet and alone. Cheerio!"

"Gosh, Bobby!" Cynthia exclaimed, staring out the window at the darkening sky. "It's snowing this minute."

"So what?" Roberta asked. "After all, as Everson pointed out, it's still March and who's afraid of a little snow? It probably won't amount to anything."

But it continued snowing all night and when Roberta was relieved next morning it was to greet a white world. The sun rose and she went to bed to the accompaniment of dripping eaves.

"I shall have the chains put on again," she told herself sleepily and knew nothing more until the alarm awoke her promptly at noon. She had allowed twenty minutes for shower and dressing, twenty minutes for breakfast which was really luncheon, and twenty minutes to get Jeremiah started. She hoped he wouldn't prove obstreperous. She gave a glance at the weather. Not too bad. Her new light tweed suit tempted her. She lifted a perky straw hat from its box and tried the effect at various angles on her bronze-brown head. Another glance out the window at the snow-covered landscape decided her. The hat went back into its box and the tweed suit to the closet. She pulled a rust colored wool over her head and fastened its wide brown suede belt about her slim waist. Her suitcase was already packed and with her short fur jacket and rakish felt hat under one arm, she hurried down to the dining room.

It was a few minutes after one o'clock when she left the annex. At the garage where she kept her car, one of the mechanics urged her to stick to the state road for if she did she would not need chains.

"The state road's almost always clear, Miss Cameron," he said, giving the windshield an extra polish. "If you have to go any distance through bad roads 'most anyone 'll put the chains on for you."

In spite of the fact she had slept barely four hours, Roberta felt rested and eager to reach Shandleys Beach and the Macklin summer home. Little Mary was five months old. Beth had written she now noticed things and that her smiles were no longer due entirely to gas on her tummy. Roberta wished they hadn't moved to the lake so early. Surely Will should have known, if Beth did not, that in March the weather is fickle. Why had they gone this year? Of course the past few days had been misleading. Even the birds had been deceived.

Spring was always lovely at the lake. Roberta didn't altogether blame Beth for wanting to watch its approach in all its gay pageantry—so wonderful—so mysterious! The most sluggish pulse must quicken to find robins and bluebirds had appeared suddenly one

[15]

morning before the snow was entirely gone. No one could remain unmoved as he watched the wild geese come out of the south in great wedges of honking animation, eager, no doubt, to reach the bird sanctuary miles farther north. And the ecstasy of discovering the first crocuses and violets beneath their protective covering of leaves! The fun of clearing the garden of winter-accumulated rubbish; watching smoke from the bonfire curl upward into the clear spring sky.

Roberta knew Will always took a week's vacation in early spring in order to get the summer place ready for occupancy. It must be because spring seemed to have arrived earlier than usual this year that Beth had decided to accompany him. She had written Roberta everything was far advanced and they would look for her any day she could get away.

It might be spring as the calendar insisted, but in spite of that, Roberta was glad she had worn her fur jacket. The heat in the car was far from adequate. She left Weston and headed north. It was good to get away for a little while. She loved her job but just the same she felt in need of a bit of change and recreation.

She stopped for a red light and scanned the sky to the north. It certainly looked far from reassuring. The wind was increasing, too. But as the garage man had said—the state roads were almost always open and she should experience no difficulty in reaching her destination. The sun continued to shine. But to the north and west the huge banks of clouds, black and menacing, were moving toward her with slow ominous precision.

A car edged into the space ahead and Roberta frowned in annoyance. Just because Jeremiah was shabby didn't mean he could be shoved aside with impunity. She would pass that shiny black coupé just as soon as the light changed. But the coupé turned down a side road and Roberta saw a red cross on its door panel.

"That's all right," she said to herself as she shifted into high and drove on. "I wonder if I would prefer public health to hospital work. I don't think so. But if the other doesn't pan out, I can always take a course in that."

She liked the idea of general hospital work—not specializing in any particular phase of it. There was even something stimulating about being on call, for instance. A nurse on call never knew just when or where she might be vitally needed—a life or death case, perhaps. There was the time she was on call and had been summoned to male medical. When she arrived she found the nurse in charge out cold and her assistant, a student like herself, in the grip of a delirious patient. She was trying to get him back into bed but he was determined to go downstairs. Roberta had been glad she was tall and strong. Between them they got the man into bed and securely strapped, then summoned the resident. It was queer about that, too, because both girls declared she had not been called—by them, at least. That must have been a case of mental telepathy.

There was always a certain fascination to hospital life. Of course nursing meant hard work; but who minded hard work if one was well and happy and sure of her vocation? Why scarcely a day—or night—passed without its interesting—often exciting occurrence. She had laughed over one incident, not because it was amusing, but because she, who was not at all timid or imaginative, had felt her flesh creep and her nerves tingle in sudden panic. It had happened this past winter. She was on night duty on a private floor. A man in the next to the last room from the end of the corridor had just died and with the assistance of the night orderly she had fixed him up and sent him down to the morgue. She was finishing his chart and preparing to go back and clean up the room when she was startled to see a red light go on outside his door. It was about two o'clock on one of those dark, sub-zero nights when wind howled and moaned; when shutters rattled and unexpected, eerie sounds—stealthy footsteps and ghostly whispers—echoed in the long dim corridor.

Her common sense told her there must be a perfectly plausible explanation but all the same it was definitely scary. She decided to wait until Phyllis Marks made her rounds with coffee and sandwiches. What she and Phyllis expected to find they didn't know but hand in hand they opened the door and entered the room. Phyllis dropped the empty tray with which she had armed herself and the two had difficulty in stifling their hysterical laughter. The bell had slipped off the bed and struck the floor in such a way as to turn on the current.

Roberta smiled again as she recalled the incident. "I wasn't really afraid," she told herself, "and I suppose if Marks hadn't appeared I should have gone in by myself, but it was the strangeness of it that upset me. It all goes to prove Dad was so very right when he used to preach fearlessness to us. 'The best way to conquer a difficulty is to face it; for a battle faced is half won.' Dear Dad," she murmured half aloud, "I miss you so!"

Thirty miles from Weston the sun disappeared. Immediately snow began to fall in eddying gusts. The state road was still bare and Roberta was glad she had decided against chains. She changed her mind, however, some miles farther on. They must have had a lot of snow up north here. Traffic continued heavy and Jeremiah complained less than usual. That was something for which to be thankful. Now if she could cut through close to the lake instead of going on to the bridge and back down to Shandleys Beach, she would strike a state road at Bramton and lop off at least ten miles. After all, it was daylight; she had plenty of gas and Jeremiah was in fine fettle.

It was after four when she arrived at Faber Corners. She slowed. It didn't look so bad. To be sure the road was traveled very little in winter but the wind from the lake often swept great patches completely bare of snow. With any luck at all she should reach Beth's somewhere around seven. On she went. The road was rutty and she sang aloud as they bumped over the miles. She could hear the boom of the breakers against the sea wall and soon came close to the lake, white-capped and angry and almost hidden from view by the swirling snow. The wind had now reached gale proportions and except for the rather steep bank on her left she could not have been sure she was in the road at all. Her watch said four-thirty. How dark it had grown! She turned on the car lights and was dismayed at the almost impenetrable curtain before her.

Jeremiah, who had been on his best behavior, suddenly began to make vigorous protests as he plowed through drift after drift.

"One more like that and I suppose you'll quit cold," the girl said aloud as they came out into a comparatively clear space. "Maybe I should have followed the advice the girls so generously donated or stopped back there to have the chains put on. We'll soon be through the worst of it—I hope. Anyway, I just had to come, Jeremiah. It's ages since I had any time off. With four whole days I couldn't pass up the chance to see the baby and the others. Now could I? And it was spring the day I decided. Oo-oh, that was a squeak, Jerry my lad, but you're doing nobly—if you only keep it up. We can't be more than five miles from Bramton road and what's five miles to you, Old Scout? Oh, darn you! Stop your groaning!" for the shabby little car was giving signs of distress.

Directly in front the wind had piled, what looked to Roberta's startled eyes, a veritable mountain of snow. She pressed her foot on the accelerator for an encouraging spurt. If she could get through this drift she might be able to make headway. Each drift conquered made one less to tackle and perhaps the road was more sheltered farther on.

Into the drift Jeremiah plunged, slewed sharply, and with a protesting sigh, quit cold with two wheels in a ditch. Roberta reversed. She must get back into the road. Perhaps another try would do it. The wheels spun. The engine coughed and died. Jeremiah refused to budge. The snow swirled in a thick cloud. The wind roared. Darkness deepened.

Roberta sat back and contemplated her plight. Why on earth had she ever attempted this short cut? The ten or a dozen miles she had saved wasn't worth considering beside the necessity of digging herself out only to get into a worse predicament if the going became worse. She ought to have had sense enough to keep to the state road. Will and Beth were crazy to come out here in March, anyway. And just why did Jeremiah choose this particular time to give up the ghost? What to do! There must be some way out of this.

Not a single house she had passed since leaving Route 20 showed signs of life. Sensible people! They knew those few spring-like days were deceptive—a storm-breeder as Tess Everson insisted. Traffic was now absolutely nil. She hadn't seen a car since she left the state road. She stared ahead. She might have been alone in an empty world. She tried the starter again. A tantalizing buzz was the only response. She opened a window and peered out. A gray depressing sight. Maybe someone would come along. Maybe she would have to stay right here until morning. Suddenly a light gleamed ahead on her left. She wondered if it might be another fool trying to buck Old Man Winter. But the light remained stationary. It was back from the road. There must be a house some two hundred yards away, as nearly as she could figure. Could anyone in that house hear her horn in this wind? If they did hear would they come to her assistance? She decided to go in person. Maybe she could borrow a shovel—or even buy one. She might even resort to theft if the other two approaches failed. She didn't dare wait any longer. It certainly wasn't getting any lighter.

She opened the car door with difficulty. She wore no galoshes and her fur coat was short. It shouldn't be hard going. She was glad she was long-legged. She must reach that light. The snow was deeper than she had thought and she was wet and panting from exertion when she reached a half-open and nearly buried gate in a low stone wall. She floundered through the snow to the small dark porch and felt around for a bell or knocker then pounded on the door with her fists. The wind howled and the snow had already covered her trail. What was the matter in there? She pounded again and rattled the doorknob.

A dog barked shrilly and a man's voice ordered him to be quiet. Roberta peered through one of the glass side panels into a dark hall. A door opened and she saw a tall man with a lamp coming toward her.

Chapter 2

ROBERTA STAMPED THE SNOW FROM HER FEET. THE GLOW caused from her exertion had faded. Her teeth chattered. She was wet and cold. The man released the catch and swung the door wide, shielding the flaming lamp with his cupped hand. The dog lunged at her, then sat down on his haunches, tail thumping the floor.

"He's just being friendly," the man said. His voice was young. He wore a dressing gown and slippers.

Roberta gasped. "Th-that's all right. I—my car is stuck down the road and I wonder if there is someone here who can help me—or lend me a shovel so I can dig it out." She pointed west. "It's back there."

"Great Jehoshaphat, girl!" the man exclaimed. "Come on in. Dig you out! In this wind it would require a steam shovel and even then it would be a case of love's labor lost. I began having trouble miles east of here and that was more than an hour ago. The drifts are worse farther east. Better make the best of it. Take off your wet things——"

"But my bag is in my car——" Roberta began, trying to keep from shaking.

"And likely to stay there for a while," the man told her. "There must be something you can put on—in one of the closets upstairs. Give me your coat and hat—I'll hang them in the kitchen where there's a fire."

Somewhat unwillingly, Roberta obeyed. This was the last straw. Old Jeremiah was now definitely headed for the last round-up. She had threatened trading him in on several occasions but kept putting it off. What if the car had been her father's? What if they two had gone on fishing and camping trips in it? She and Jeremiah had positively reached the parting of the ways. She had been sentimental far too long. Jeremiah, with his predilection for getting her into a jam when she least expected it, had pulled his last boner. She took a step toward the steep narrow stairs.

"Wait," her host said. "I'll bring another lamp. Fortunately, they are all clean and full of oil. The electricity seems to be off—the storm, I suppose. My respect and admiration for the owner of this place grows by leaps and bounds. What a gal!"

"Then you——" began Roberta.

"Oh, I don't own it," the man said. "It was loaned us—me——" He hesitated and went on grimly: "My plans—er—fell through and I came back for my bags.

[25]

Fortunately I got here before the storm completely blocked the roads."

He went down the hall leaving Roberta in total darkness. Was he here alone? Before she could do more than merely wonder about it, he was back with two lighted lamps, one of which he handed her. She began a slow ascent of the stairs but paused as he went on:

"I'll rustle something hot. Soup—canned. There's no hot water so a bath is out; but you might try a brisk rub with a rough towel. There are plenty in the linen closet near the bathroom. Make yourself entirely at home. My name is Baxter—Chris Baxter, very much at your service."

"I am Roberta Cameron, Mr. Baxter, and—and—thank you. I—there seems nothing else for me to do." She ran down the stairs again. "How long do you think it will be before——"

"The snowplow gets through? I haven't the least idea, Miss Cameron," he said regretfully. "You probably noticed this road isn't a much traveled one in winter. I was warned in Bramton against coming here this afternoon. I imagine no plow will make any attempt until the storm is over. But don't worry. Spring snowstorms are usually short-lived——"

"But I—I am due at my sister's—Mrs. Macklin—tonight. Is there a telephone?"

"There is, but it must be disconnected or out of

order. I couldn't raise Central a while back. I'm extremely sorry. This is what Insurance Companies call an act of God. There seems to be nothing we can do about it except be thankful we are inside and more or less comfortable. Now run along and change into dry things—stockings, anyway."

"You are very kind," Roberta murmured and went upstairs. "Well," she said to herself as she slipped out of her wet frock, "this is a nice how-do-you-do. This man seems all right—trying to put me at ease. Young, not too good-looking; lean and sort of weather-beaten. An outdoor man—probably a traveling salesman or maybe an insurance agent. I hope he's married and crazy about his wife. Not that it will make any difference to me. I can take care of myself; but I should dislike having to be unpleasant after accepting his hospitality—or rather, that of the owners, whoever they are."

She had entered a room near the head of the stairs. It was small and contained a single bed, cretonne-skirted dressing table, one comfortable chair and little else. Amid the heterogeneous accumulation on shelves and hooks in the closet she discovered faded slacks, a clean knitted pullover that had undoubtedly once been white, and a pair of very scuffed brown oxfords. There were several stockings in one of the drawers—none mates; but she found socks turned one in the other and gratefully pulled them on her icy feet. Evidently someone in the owner's family was about her size. She rubbed her damp, short hair until every curl shone and wondered what Miss Longworth would say if she should see her now. But just what else could she have done? After all, she was not a child, and she had no intention of letting her imagination make a coward of her.

Something smelled heavenly—a mixture of coffee and spices. She hadn't realized she was hungry. She picked up the lamp and went down the stairs, hesitating as she reached the last step.

"Come in here," a voice called and Roberta followed it down the hall to what proved to be the kitchen. "I'm an artist with a can opener," Chris Baxter told her. Roberta noticed he had exchanged the dressing gown for a coat and he now wore shoes. "I hope you are going to like this soup."

"I'm sure I shall, Mr. Baxter——"

"Oh, call me Chris and I'll call you Roberta—no, let's make it Robin. Sort of suits you. Mind? Good girl!" as Roberta shook her head. "Might as well be friends while we're isolated. There's a lot of stuff in the cellar food closet so we won't starve. And I suggest we eat out here where it's warm. I like a kitchen— always have since I was a kid. Smell good, don't they? We can have a fire in the living-room grate, too." He eyed her approvingly. "What did you do with your wet clothes?"

"Hung them around," she told him. "I suppose I chose the daughter's room—if there is a daughter."

"No. Meta and Jim haven't been married very long—two or three years, maybe. No doubt the guest room. Probably Grace stays here summers. She's Meta's sister—lives in New York. Radio. I don't remember what program she's on. Here, let me ——" as she drew a chair nearer the table.

Over the appetizing soup the two surreptitiously appraised each other and gradually the feeling of strangeness left Roberta. She relaxed and listened with amusement to her host's tales of adventure. Christopher Baxter was an engineer and north for a brief important consultation with his chief. He was leaving the next week for another two years in Peru, by which time his job should be completed.

"Doesn't your family hate your being so far away?" Roberta asked, feeling she must say something.

Chris shook his head. "No family—except Hilda, my sister, married and living in Spokane. No, I have no family—nor likely to have—now." For a moment his likable face seemed to harden. The laugh that followed almost at once had no mirth in it. "You've heard that old saw: 'He travels fastest who travels alone'? If that's true, I should break all speed records."

"I'm sorry," the girl murmured sympathetically.

"Don't be," he said quickly. "At that, I'm far from alone in the world. I have a doctor uncle—a swell old chap—and a mighty sweet cousin. Oh, yes, and there's a miscellaneous lot, varying in degrees of relationship. Meta Palmer's one. How about you, Robin?"

"I have a brother, Neil, in England—a war correspondent, and my sister, Beth, Mrs. Macklin. That's all except for a few cousins scattered about. There's nothing interesting or spectacular about me."

"Can you cook? You can? Then, lady, you're both interesting and spectacular and if you can make biscuits and brown gravy *sans* lumps, you're a marvel. How about it?"

"Of course," Roberta told him calmly. "That's easy."

"Think so? Well, I can brew a cup of coffee fit for the gods; and man, can I make griddle cakes to melt in your mouth! But biscuits——" He shook his head. "And there's no butter in this menage and nary an egg. We—I was supposed to provide them, you see. But we have a variety of canned stuff. Milk, meat, fish, crackers, puddings, all sorts of pickles, jellies and fruits, but no eggs and no butter. I yearn for butter. I'm a fiend for butter, but we just haven't any, so if you'll concoct gravy—a lot of gravy to go with canned veal, it will be swell. I dumped out the meat—thought I'd warm it and eat as is—*and then you came!*" He said it fervently and Roberta thought:

"How men love food!" She felt quite at home, now. Why, this Chris Baxter was just like Neil—always

[30]

hungry. It would be fun fixing things for him. "Is there flour?" she asked.

"Sure, in that bin over there. Help yourself. Sa-ay, listen to the wind! Am I glad we're inside! Pity the homeless on a night like this. I'll make a fire in the living room. If you want me for anything, just call."

Roberta hummed softly as she made biscuits and popped them into the oven. The veal was heating nicely and the jelly from it was going to make delicious gravy. She set the table with the pretty china she found in one of the cupboards—really the Palmers had excellent taste—and prepared to call her host.

She made a grimace as she thought of the hospital and the strict rules governing student nurses. She had reported her impending visit to her sister but had failed to notify Beth the exact time of her arrival. It would be pretty hard to make Miss Longworth understand the present situation—this being stranded in a strange house whose sole other occupant was a young and attractive man. Ye gods! She could visualize the superintendent's steely blue eyes if she were called upon to explain. No doubt if it came to an issue she would be disgraced for life. Yet how perfectly silly! She couldn't remain in the car. She would freeze to death though maybe the hospital heads might think it preferable to the present situation. Piffle! She had no patience with people who were such sticklers for stupid conventions—conventions that somehow managed to make one self-conscious and killed all joy in perfectly innocent adventures.

Chris answered her call with flattering alacrity.

"Lady, you have saved my life!" he exclaimed as he surveyed the attractively set table with its steaming food. "That blasted chimney smokes like the deuce."

"And you an engineer——" began Roberta. With startling suddenness came the raucous summons of a horn.

"What—who's that?" Roberta's gaze flew to Chris's face. "Maybe it's the owners——"

"Of course it isn't. They go to Florida every winter and remain until May. I'll get my flashlight. It may be one of the neighbors. Shut up, Rufus, and stay back. Close the door, Robin. I don't want him dashing out into the storm."

Roberta strained her ears. Chris was talking to a man who seemed to be shouting and laughing a great deal. The front door slammed and footsteps hurried down the hall. Chris came into the kitchen, a worried look in his eyes. He stood for a moment studying Roberta's flushed face then blurted out:

"This is the very devil of a thing to happen. I wonder just how game you are, Robin. Would you lie and stick to it if you—well—if the need arose? I have a hunch you would. Listen. That was a fellow I knew in Princeton—not intimately—God forbid! His wife and my sister were in school together though I don't think they've kept in touch. They are out front and want to spend the night here. I had to tell them they could. What else? Now listen, Robin. Bert's one of those subnormal creatures possessed of an unwholesome mind—dotes on scandal and unsavory stories. He thinks he's witty. Needless to say, I don't. I told him *my wife* and I would be glad to put them up. Believe me, it seemed the only thing to do. It doesn't matter about me—but you! You believe that? You must. You're taking no chances—are perfectly safe. I had to do it. Here, put this on ——" He dipped two fingers into a vest pocket and brought out a small plain gold ring. "It was to have been my wife's—but there is to be no wife. Do you understand? Good! We are spending a few days here—for a rest—before going back to Orellana. The living room's full of smoke, but it will soon go off—I hope. Don't be scared—it will be all right. I'll see to that. There they are now."

Chapter 3

As the door closed behind Chris, Roberta stared about her in consternation. After all, she didn't know this Chris Baxter from Adam's off ox, except that a little while ago she would have been willing to stake her life on his being a decent sort. Now she felt trapped—helpless—hedged about with difficulties. She turned the ring round and round on her finger. Who did he think he was that he could do this to her and what sort of girl did he believe her to be? A voice called from the hall.

"Robin, darling—come welcome the wayfarers."

Roberta lingered a moment but there seemed nothing for her to do but play the game as Chris had outlined, so with chin up but knees far from steady, she opened the door and went down the hall to the living room, Rufus sniffing at her heels. Chris came to meet her. He laid his arm across her shoulders.

"My dear, this is Mrs. Tildon and her husband. We

were just about to sit down to dinner, Bert—a snack in the kitchen. Robin and I ran away for a few days' rest. We go back next week." His arm pressed reassuringly. "Shall I show them to a room, dear?" he asked. "Or perhaps you know where you want to put them. I'm sorry about this fire. The chimney must be damp." He removed his arm but took her hand in his. The wedding ring was like a circle of fire on her finger. "We arrived only this afternoon so haven't had a chance to do much," he explained. "Fortunately, we beat the storm. I'll set two more places and when you are ready, dinner will be served."

Roberta thought: "Oh, yes. You can be affable and hospitable. You know these people and you're probably a better liar than I am. Darn you, Jeremiah! It's the junk yard for you. And I'll not turn a hair."

Mrs. Tildon was making an attempt to strangle a cough with her handkerchief but her husband coughed raucously.

"It's not as bad as all that!" Roberta thought indignantly; but she took the lamp Chris handed her and said with what she hoped was gracious hospitality: "If you will come with me, the air will at least be free from smoke."

Which room held Chris's things? She would have to chance it. After all, neither of the newcomers suspected anything amiss—at least she hoped not—and would not recognize slips should she make any. She opened a door at the head of the stairs and closed it quickly. A nursery. Chris had said the owners were childless. Had it all been lies? Then —— No use wondering. She must carry on, now. If she attempted any explaining the whole affair would take on a lurid aspect. She led the way along the hall to what she felt sure must be the master bedroom. The open door revealed twin beds and plain but adequate furnishings. She placed the lamp on the dresser. Mrs. Tildon sank into a chair. The wooden shutters were still closed and Roberta threw them back. Was the storm abating? A gust of wind swirled snow into her face and she hastily shut the window. The room was very cold.

"The storm seems to have disrupted everything," she explained. "But we don't mind lamps or candles for the short time we shall be here. In fact, it's rather fun. I'll get fresh linen." Lucky she knew where the linen closet was. Chris had placed a lighted lamp in the lower hall and by its faint illumination she sorted out the necessary sheets and pillow slips.

"I suppose this is your summer home," Mrs. Tildon ventured as Roberta returned with the bedding.

"Oh no. It belongs to some distant relative of Chris. It's quiet and so ——"

"I hope you don't mind our barging in on you like this," Mrs. Tildon said apologetically, then after a moment: "I didn't know Chris was married although I heard he was engaged. Hilda and I have been out of touch, late years. You know we were in school together."

"Yes, I know you were," Roberta replied, glad Chris had told her.

"I never met your husband, Mrs. Baxter; but I had a terrible crush on him when I was in school. He isn't as good-looking as his picture," she said bluntly and a puzzled look came into her eyes. "Funny, but I didn't think the name of Chris's fiancée was —— What did he call you?"

"Oh—oh. What a tangled web we weave——" Roberta thought as she smoothed fresh slips on pillows. "Chris calls me Robin for some reason," she replied, hoping the inquisitive little lady would be satisfied with this explanation.

"Oh," she said. "Cute. Have you been married long?"

Roberta hoped she wasn't blushing. She murmured: "Not long," and moved toward the door. "You may have a fire here if you like and we can heat water if you want a bath. We haven't started the furnace yet."

"Don't bother," the other said. "We shall probably leave first thing in the morning or as soon as this storm is over. I'm not actually wet—only cold. Bert carried me in from the car. If he had used his head instead of taking Ben's advice to cut through this impossible road just to save a few wretched miles we'd have at least reached Wamsley and could no doubt have gone straight through to Syracuse. Short cut indeed! I hate detours!"

Roberta murmured: "You and me both!"

"I'm sorry," Mrs. Tildon said. "I didn't hear what you said."

"This is probably a very good road in summer," Roberta explained.

"I suppose so. Please, Mrs. Baxter, no dinner for us. We had a late lunch and a rather hearty tea before we left Bramton. I really couldn't eat a thing and Bert should not. I believe I shall take an aspirin and lie down for a bit. My head feels sort of muzzy."

As she left the room, Roberta closed the door behind her. From downstairs came the voices of the two men. Suddenly another sound reached her. She ran to the hall window. The snowplow!

Bert Tildon came up the stairs two steps at a time.

"Come on, Marge," he called. "We can go on—follow the plow."

He hadn't seen Roberta and she heard them congratulating each other on getting out of this dump so quickly.

"Baxter always was more or less of a stuffed shirt," Bert growled. "Felt himself above the common herd. I'm darn glad not to be under obligations to him. Must have come down in the world to be willing to spend his honeymoon in a God-forsaken hole like this. Hurry up, Marge. That road will fill again if this wind doesn't go down. We may not be so lucky next time."

"So it's a honeymoon I'm supposed to be enjoying," Roberta smiled ironically. "A fine honeymoon!" She called a good-bye from the top of the stairs then hurriedly changed into her still damp clothes.

Armed with shovels, Chris and Bert made a narrow path to the road and the Tildon car. Mrs. Tildon followed. Lights gleamed through the lessening storm and they were gone. The front door slammed once more and Chris called:

"Robin, where are you? Come on down and eat while things are at least warm."

Roberta picked up the lamp and hurried downstairs.

"I'm going, too, Chris," she told him as she pulled on her coat.

"Good Lord, why the rush?" he demanded. "Here's this swell meal all ready. Surely you can stay and help eat it, and you're liable to catch your death in those wet clothes."

"I can't. Honestly, Chris, I must get to my sister's. She'll be ——" She stopped. Beth didn't know she was coming tonight. But just the same —— She looked up at the tall young man eyeing her so disapprovingly and laughed. "Being stranded here was no doubt due to an act of God as you said, Chris; but staying on when the way of escape is made possible would be tempting Providence altogether too much." She reached for her hat. "I'm grateful and I wish you a pleasant trip south and loads of luck!"

He caught her hand. "Tell me," he urged, "where I can get in touch with you. You've been a pal, Robin, and I——"

"Our paths aren't at all likely to cross again," Roberta told him, surprised and a little dismayed at her feeling of regret. "And it really wasn't a bit necessary to tell that utterly fantastic story—to—resort to such—well—outmoded chivalry. I am entirely capable of taking care of myself."

"But you don't know the Tildons as I do——" he began.

"Nor likely to. In spite of what people say to the contrary, Chris, the world is a huge place and we'll never meet. I must go before the road fills again. Let me take your shovel. I'll leave it at the gate." She opened the door and turned for a last good-bye. She ought not to feel sorry at going, but she was.

Chris followed. He silently cleared the snow from the bogged down car and Roberta settled herself behind the steering wheel. Apparently the rest had done Jeremiah good. The engine turned over at once and, with a healthy shove from Chris, the car heaved itself out of the shallow rut. Roberta opened the door and leaned out.

"You've been very kind, Chris, and I am truly grateful."

He came close to her.

"Somehow I have a hunch we shall meet again, Roberta Cameron," he said soberly. "Until then, *adios*."

Jeremiah's wheels spun helplessly for a moment, found traction and lurched forward. Roberta lifted a hand in farewell and sped on her way, praying silently that this time Jeremiah would get her safely through.

It wasn't until she was removing her damp clothes in her room at the Macklins' an hour later that she noticed the ring still on the third finger of her left hand.

"Oh, my good gosh!" she exclaimed, hastily slipping it off. "What an idiot! What must he think of me? Why didn't he remind me?"

She turned it over and over in her hand, examining it curiously. Such a plain wedding ring for a bride of today. No diamonds, no engraving. Just a thin, plain gold band. Nothing inside either. She must stop on her way back and return it. She wrapped it in tissue paper and dropped it into her purse.

"Wife for an hour!" she murmured to herself as she prepared to join the others downstairs. "What a perfectly crazy and entirely uncalled for thing to do! But just the same, I like you, Chris Baxter."

Chapter 4

ROBERTA MADE NO MENTION OF THE TILDONS; OF POSING as Chris Baxter's wife or of the ring reposing in her purse, when she related her adventure to Beth and Will. Chris had been telling the truth after all when he said the place belonged to the Palmers. Beth knew the cottage but not the owners. Will knew Jim Palmer, having played golf with him at the Bramton Country Club.

"But you did a crazy thing trying to cut across there, Bob," her brother-in-law scolded. "No one uses that road in winter. I have never known of a single place being occupied from November to mid-April, at least, until this year—if then. It's pretty bleak—gets the full sweep of wind straight from Medicine Hat."

"But this is supposed to be spring, Will," Roberta reminded him.

"Supposed to be is right. Those few mild days fooled everyone it seems, even your sister. It was lucky for you the plow went through. It must be that some of the cottages are open else the County wouldn't have bothered. The Palmer house is about halfway along. A bit farther on you'd have reached the Austin place— they're always the first to arrive and probably they, too, thought winter was over. You could have spent the night with them."

"I wouldn't have stayed after the plow went through. I wanted to get here. Anyway, I couldn't go another foot in Jeremiah just at that time. As it was I was soaked when I reached the Palmer front door. Lucky for me someone happened to be there or I would probably be in for a bout with pneumonia—a heavy cold at least."

"Fortunately, the occupant was a decent sort," Will reminded her. "You take altogether too many chances, Bob. You might have let yourself in for a lot of unpleasantness—or worse."

Roberta laughed derisively. "Honestly, Will, one would think I was ten instead of twenty-one. I assure you I am perfectly capable of taking care of myself. We learn how to do that while we are in training if we don't know how before we enter." She tousled his smooth red hair affectionately.

"Oh, don't fuss, Will," Beth chided. "Nowadays girls are absolutely fearless. And remember, I'm going to see to it that Mary is just as independent as her Aunt Bob is. Where did you acquire all those antiquated ideas about girls, darling? I bet I know. From your Grandmother Macklin. That's what comes of being brought up by contemporaries of Victoria. If your mother had lived, your knowledge of the female of the species would be vastly broader. I wonder if all southern men still cling to the idea women are fragile creatures to be kept in cotton and treated as if they were not quite bright."

"What brought that up?" her husband asked, reaching for the evening paper. "And I'm no longer a southerner, my dear. You told me yourself I had lost most of my southern mannerisms and that I was as shrewd a lawyer as any Yankee. Let it go at that."

Beth left the room to help Prunella in the kitchen. Roberta stretched her feet to the roaring fire in the grate and leaned back in the comfortable chair. She was tired and hungry and hoped dinner wasn't too far off. She surveyed her surroundings with approving eyes. Such a lovely room! Long and not too narrow with windows filling the entire wall facing the lake. The ceiling and walls were paneled in dark oak. Well-filled bookcases flanked the fireplace and rugs and furnishings blended to make the room restful and attractive. She had always liked this house better than the one in Corinth which was much larger. Ever since the death of her parents she had thought of it as home. Beth was nearly six years her senior and had been married seven years before Mary, their five-months-old daughter, was born. Roberta stole a glance at her brother-in-law and met his gaze above his paper. They smiled companionably at each other and Roberta said:

"You're not really worried about me, are you, Will?"

"Of course not," he answered. "That is, not usually. But I wish you wouldn't simply dash into things the way you do, without a thought as to consequences. You know you're an extremely lovely young girl, my dear."

"Thanks," Roberta said, stifling a yawn. "And what has that to do with the price of beef—if anything? I mean, I'm glad I'm not too hard on the eyes, of course; but truly I can take care of myself. Wait until your daughter begins to show her individuality and assert her independence, Will. Then you'll have something to keep you really occupied. Have you quite forgotten I'm a trained nurse—or almost? If you knew of some of the situations we have to come up against, you would realize our training fits us to meet life bravely and efficiently. I could tell you some things that would startle you, to say the least, but I won't."

"I don't doubt it," Will growled. "I never wanted you to be a nurse in the first place. It wasn't at all necessary. Your home is with us—what we have is yours. Now that you are nearly through training, just what do you plan on doing? Private work? Public health?"

Roberta smiled at him. He was such a dear! "It's rather a coincidence, Will, but I was pondering that very thing as I drove over this afternoon. I think I shall stick to hospital work if I can get into one that suits me. I thought I would send for information and decide while I am on vacation this summer."

"And you are not thinking of marrying? Isn't there someone ——" he began.

Roberta shook her head emphatically. "You know, Will, I don't seem to fall very hard for your sex. Oh, they're all right—but—well, I haven't, to date, met any man with whom I long to spend the rest of my life. I suppose we get sort of fed up with men after we've listened to their grunts and snorts night and day for weeks on end. It's a wonder to me a nurse ever marries—especially a man she has once nursed. She has seen him when he needed a shave and a haircut, cleaned up after he has spilled his food over an immaculate sheet and soothed him when he fussed over trifles and rebelled at fate and life in general. I assure you I experience no thrill while I'm brushing a man's teeth or changing his bed. His wife may be able to keep her love intact while doing the necessary, personal things for him, but, definitely, not his nurse. She does it because that's her job—that's what she's trained to do. She does it to make the patient more comfortable; not because of any emotional upheaval he may have brought to her well-disciplined heart."

Will's face was amused. "How about doctors? Nurses often marry doctors, don't they?"

"Not this nurse." Roberta wrinkled her nose in distaste. "Doctors! Ugh! I loathe the creatures. No, Will, I'll never give you a doctor for a brother-in-law. Conceited things! They make me sick! What have they got to be so cocky over? Nine times out of ten it's due to the nurse's care the patient recovers and not to the doctor. In my opinion, doctors are very greatly overrated. Of course they have their uses—surgeons especially; but personally, I don't care for them."

Will Macklin laughed. "You're still a child, Bobby," he said affectionately. "The right man hasn't appeared yet. When he does it won't make the slightest difference whether he's a rich man, poor man, beggar man, thief—doctor, lawyer, merchant or chief. You'll see."

"He will have to be as nice as you are, Will," Roberta murmured, slipping her arm through his as they answered the summons from the dining room.

Chapter 5

WHEN ROBERTA AWOKE NEXT MORNING, THE SUN WAS shining and a robin sang outside her window. His song wasn't especially ecstatic, but what could one expect with not an inch of ground bare of snow? The sun was warm and probably the snow would melt rapidly, but it was very heavy and some time must elapse before the good brown earth would be again visible. The roads, however, were quite clear and dry on the day she returned to the hospital and she made good time. She felt rested and happy.

The sudden changes in the weather had brought about a lot of sickness in and around Weston just as Tess had predicted. Sufferers from colds, influenza, pneumonia and other ills filled the hospital to capacity. It was well into May before conditions moderated and doctors and nurses had a breathing spell. During the whole of that time Roberta had been on night duty— she was still on it. Well, it would soon be over. Just a few weeks and she would be at Shandleys Beach, state examinations safely past and her R.N. assured.

She was still in bed one afternoon, dreaming of the future—trying to decide whether to wait until fall before sending in applications for a position, as Will and Beth advised, or to do so immediately after graduation. Two or three weeks would be sufficient vacation. She was tired now, to be sure, but a few days of lying about in the sun—of doing absolutely nothing—would be about all she felt she needed or wanted. Her door burst open.

" Bobby Cameron, I'm the luckiest girl in the world," Helen Donley cried, waving a letter before Roberta's eyes and plopping down on the bed beside her. " I've got a job—a grand one! "

" Good for you! Where? Let me move over—you'll be more comfortable. There! "

" You remember the old curmudgeon I had up in male medical so long last winter—the one with the infected gall bladder? Oh, you do too. His granddaughter raised ruction because we put a NO VISITORS sign on his door and the floor nurse wouldn't make an exception in her case. Don't you remember she threatened to take him home and Longworth dared her to try it? Oh, I see light begins to percolate at last. Well, I've been offered the job taking care of him. The granddaughter—let's see, her name's Martha Cooke—says her grandfather spoke well of my care and wishes me to continue as his nurse—indefinitely. Isn't that a break? You know who they are, don't you?"

Roberta shook her head, looking puzzled. She had been so busy she had only the foggiest memories of last winter.

"Honestly, you're a goop, Cameron," Helen exclaimed in disgust. "Don't you ever try to keep up with world affairs? He's Baldwin's Bitters."

Roberta rolled over on her face and choked with laughter. "'Baldwin's Bitters—For Unruly Livers,'" she gurgled. "Has he been taking his own medicine, Donley? Is that what's the matter with the old duffer?"

"Probably," the other grinned, "but that's beside the point. The man's worth millions. Just think, Bob, I'll live in that swank mansion and travel with him whenever he feels the urge. I'll meet plenty of smart people and who knows but he may leave me something when he passes on?"

"No one knows, of course," Roberta agreed, "but I wouldn't bank on it. And what about the granddaughter? From all accounts she's a hellion. What's the matter with her, anyway?"

"I heard her fiancé jilted her—couldn't stand her snooty airs. But I'm not afraid of her. Haven't I a bunch of first-class ancestors somewhere in my background? I don't have to take anything from any Baldwin's Bitters heiress—for that matter, no R.N. does.

She's certainly not at all attractive and her manners are simply atrocious. But that's no skin off my elbow, darling. It's Grandpa I'm interested in."

Roberta sat up and hugged her knees. "You have my blessing, Helen," she said, "and I hope Grandpa leaves you a cool million."

"What are you going to do, Bob?" the other asked. "Stay on here? I heard Longworth offered you a job."

Roberta shook her head. "I'm looking around," she said. "I want to get into a hospital with some really big man—some surgeon who does things."

"Why not P.G. work then—Johns Hopkins or The Presbyterian or even a course in Columbia as long as money's no object?"

"Money is an object, Helen. That's why I'm not going to do P.G. I expect to get the experience and be paid at the same time. I'm going to send some applications during the summer and see what I draw."

"Weston's not so bad, Bob."

"I know it; but I want someone bigger than Arnold. Anyway, I'm interested in surgery—brain, spine—oh, you know, unusual operations, and we get little of that sort of thing here."

"Well, you've got to hand it to Arnold, Bob," Helen said. "With all his faults he knows his limitations. Some surgeons would tackle a brain job and bungle it in preference to advising another hospital or at least another surgeon. In a way, Arnold's big, you know."

[51]

"I know; but just the same I'm not staying on."

"Don't think I'm mad about Arnold, Bob," Helen went on. "There's something of the butcher in him— something in the avidity with which he approaches an operation that turns my blood to ice water. No doubt you've felt it, too. And in spite of his success—he is successful, you know, Bob—I dislike the man."

"I know," Roberta repeated, "and it isn't that especially, and I feel the same way you do about Arnold. I'm interested in something besides straight sure-of-the-results surgery. I really am, Helen. That's why I said brain."

"Sure-of-the-results, Bob? No one can be sure. The simplest operation may prove——"

"I know," Roberta hastened to explain, "I meant the operation itself."

Helen laughed cynically. "The operation was a success but the patient failed to rally."

"Exactly. No doubt the patient would have died anyway. The human element must always be taken into consideration. What I am trying to say is: I am keen about watching a real surgeon perform a miracle."

"You're welcome. Give me a nice long, not too obstreperous chronic. Oh, hello, Everson! I hear you're going back to Nova Scotia. Well, you always were a hardy soul. I guess nearly all in the class are placed, aren't they?"

"I imagine so—all but one or two. What about you,

Bob? Staying on? I heard you have the chance," Tess repeated.

" No, I'm not staying on. I'm taking a vacation first and then I'm going into some hospital—I don't know just where, yet," Roberta replied.

" Come home with me," Tess suggested. " You'd love it up there and I can guarantee you'll find plenty to do."

Helen took Tess's arm and drew her toward the door. " You Canucks got brains? " she asked. " 'Cause if you ain't, Cameron won't be interested. It's brains she yearns to study, Tess."

The two departed, laughing. Roberta reached for her mules and went down the hall to the showers. What was so strange about her interest in brains and brain surgery? Was it because the percentage of successful operations was still by no means large? She didn't know.

Outside, the May world was riotous with color. Along the fence iris flamed purple, mauve and gold. Lilacs were already beginning to lose their first fresh lavender; but peonies were unfolding green calyxes and down the avenue the horse-chestnuts flaunted their long creamy pendants. Birds sang lustily and the air was filled with the heady perfume of growing things. Roberta paused at her window to breathe deeply. It was good to be alive—to be young and healthy on a day like this.

[53]

Four-thirty. She had time for a walk to the Park before dinner. She needed to get away for a while. She had slept late this afternoon—later than was her custom; but she had had a bad night and was exhausted when the day nurse relieved her at seven. Esther Wyman in 306b had taken a turn for the worse. Of course they had all known from the very first she hadn't a chance in the world. She had been a beautiful girl, slim and shapely, before an edema got in its distorting work. Her fiancé had been with her during the evening and Roberta's heart contracted with pity as she listened to the low murmur of their voices. Esther had come to the hospital so confident the rest and treatment would bring a complete cure of her rheumatic heart. She had told Roberta all about her approaching marriage and the house Roger was building for her. She was so very much in love and so happy about the future that the nurses found it difficult to listen unmoved.

Roberta sighed. Life could be cruel and tragic as well as beautiful. She dressed quickly and slipped out the back way. She wanted to be alone. Few people were in the Park and she found a bench in a secluded corner near the small artificial lake. Seven white swans sailed past, leaving not a ripple on the blue surface. She thought whimsically: "Fancy having one's throat compared to that of a swan!"

Across the lake two Park gardeners were busy setting

out geraniums. Occasionally one of the men reached into his jacket pocket and brought out a cracker or a crust of bread which he broke and scattered on the water. Immediately there was a rush of ducks and swans in that direction and then, after a hectic minute, they would all return to other business—the man to his planting and the ducks and swans to grubbing in shallow water along the shore.

It was all very restful and Roberta sat relaxed, absorbing the quiet beauty of the day. Spireas wore bridal white and, half hidden in the grass, violets lifted their blue gaze to the sky. An oriole sang from the giant elm towering above the snowy rest house. Came a flutter of wings and a robin dropped down nearby. With a great show of busyness he accumulated bits of straw and string with which to build a love-nest. Roberta's eye followed the path of his flight with his booty. Each time he swayed on a branch for a moment, a wary eye on the landscape, then darted into the leafy heart of the old apple tree whose gnarled and twisted branches were hidden beneath a mantle of loveliness.

Back came the swans in single file like sailboats on parade. A stone splashed suddenly. A small boy shouted and a policeman came hurrying down the path. The swans with raucous cries of terror or anger and no regard for grace, half flew, half swam away from shore. The spell was broken. Roberta rose to her feet. Time to go back to the hospital. But she felt refreshed and strengthened. She had need of extra strength, for it was on that night Esther Wyman died.

Of course her death was expected—her fiancé had been told earlier in the day that it was a matter of hours; but he couldn't believe it and when it was all over, he was like a man possessed. He screamed at the doctors to do something—Esther couldn't die—he wouldn't let her. The resident shook his head, urged him to pull himself together, and departed. Roberta tried to quiet him but he pushed her angrily away. She was surprised when he went limp and slumped to the floor. She dropped to her knees beside him while Gene Graham, the interne, after a brief examination, prepared to follow the resident from the room.

"Can't take it, eh?" he said cynically.

Roberta glared at him. She loathed internes.

"Everyone isn't as hard-boiled as you are," she said coldly. "They were to have been married next week—their house is ready and waiting and—and she will never see it." Her voice caught. This was love—the real thing.

"So what?" the interne asked. "He's well out of it. If she had lived she'd have been just a drag on him. The girl was born with that heart. He ought to be thankful it ended as it did."

"Sez you!" she retorted, bitterly.

Roger opened his eyes and stared about in bewilderment.

"Take it easy," Roberta advised him gently. "Don't try to move for a moment."

His face changed—hardened. He got slowly and unsteadily to his feet.

"So," he said with deadly calm, "you couldn't save her. What good are hospitals, anyway? She trusted you and you betrayed her. Damn the lot of you!" He brushed his hand across his eyes then stared for a moment at the still figure on the bed. Roberta laid a sympathetic hand on his arm but he shook it off and without another word rushed from the room.

"Nice sort of chap," Graham remarked as he walked toward the door. "Maybe the gal's better off, too."

Roberta ignored him. Why was it, she wondered, internes were so often either fresh or hard-boiled? Or did it just so happen Weston General always drew those brands? She hoped her next case wouldn't tear at her heartstrings as this one had. It wasn't so hard to watch the aged and world-weary die; but Esther was a girl no older than she was. She had so much to live for—such a bright future. And yet, in her heart, Roberta knew, in this instance, death had come as a friend.

She wondered about Roger Hilton. He had appeared a pleasant, steady chap and she hoped he wouldn't do anything foolish. After all, it was something to have been loved as Esther loved him. All his life he would have that to remember. For some reason her thoughts turned to Chris Baxter. What had happened to his wedding plans? She had puzzled over it more than once. Had the girl jilted him for another? She felt certain she hadn't died. His tone had been too bitter when he spoke of his broken plans. But Chris Baxter wasn't the type of man to go to pieces because of a disappointment no matter how bitter.

Chapter 6

Roberta came into the corridor after settling her
two most obstreperous patients for the night. It was
ten o'clock and the ward was at last quiet. It had been
a rather hectic evening. It seemed as if every one of the
twenty-nine women in the ward held a reception. Such
a clatter of tongues in diverse languages! The two junior
students found it all very amusing and tried to carry
on a conversation with each other in Hog-Latin. They
were bright young girls—chums from childhood and
found everything in the hospital subjects for burlesque.
Reprimand had brief and only slight dampening effect.
Most of the graduate nurses side-stepped their services,
but the senior students rather enjoyed their unquench-
able spirits, knowing that all too soon they would quiet
down.

Little black-eyed Rosa Marchita, her cap over one
ear, was running up and down the corridor pushing
Carol Salvini who, a pillow held against her flat

stomach, lolled at ease *à la* Mrs. Fromento. Mrs. Rucca
Fromento considered she had prior claim on each
nurse's attention. She was the first to waken in the
morning, ready for her early ablutions, and the last to
settle for the night after she had swallowed her buttermilk. Not that she liked buttermilk—she loathed all
kinds of milk, but was determined to take everything
handed out. She was ninety pounds overweight, talka-
tive, abusive, arrogant and should have been in a private
room with special nurses. She wanted everyone to
know she could well afford such luxuries but had no
intention of wasting her Rucca's good money on any
hospital.

The nurses smiled among themselves, being fully
aware the extras she thought went free with ward
nursing would appear on the bill rendered her Rucca
upon her discharge. And Rucca Fromento, small, hard-
working and mild as his wife was stormy, priding
himself on being a good American would pay promptly
in spite of his wife's loud cries of protest. The other
women in the ward listened in disgust as she complained of everything. Hospitals were run just so doctors and nurses could experiment on people. It was the
hospital ought to pay. Nurses were all lazy and doctors
quacks. Why, her mother had brought fifteen children
into the world without any doctor butting in. She
wouldn't have had a doctor either if she had had her
way; but that Rucca—his head was full of crazy

notions—he made her have a doctor. When the last baby was delivered dead, as were the previous six, the doctor made her stay in bed instead of going out on the muck to help her Rucca, and what happened? She rolled out of bed and broke her hip. Bah! Doctors! If she had been out on the muck as she should have been she wouldn't have rolled out of bed. On and on she went—day after day.

The hip was slow in knitting. Here it was nearly June and she was only now able to be moved in a chair on wheels. Well, the nurses might as well be pushing her about as doing nothing all day. The solarium was all right but she wasn't going to be put up there and left. No, sir. She wanted to be kept moving.

Rosa and Carol were happy to be changed to night duty. At least it cut out pushing the huge Fromento over miles of roof. They liked being with Roberta. She never bawled them out when they made a slip and was always willing to help. Some of the nurses slid out of doing their share and the younger students often felt abused.

As Roberta entered the corridor, the wheel chair caught her squarely at the knees and she sat down on Carol's pillow-reinforced lap. Laughing gleefully, Rosa sped down the length of the corridor before Roberta could brake the wheels and stop the wild ride. She was flushed and somewhat annoyed. Suppose the night supervisor had appeared. It would have meant a reprimand for them all but especially for her. She was in charge.

Abject in their apologies, the culprits clasped her one on either side. They straightened her cap and smoothed down her immaculate uniform and led her to a chair in front of the desk. There they seated her with a great show of care and respect. Roberta couldn't repress her laughter at the look of mock concern on the girls' faces.

"Listen, you monkeys," she scolded, "if you don't cut out all this horseplay you're both going to get into trouble. After all," she went on, "this is a hospital you know, not an amusement hall. Honestly, girls, what on earth ever made you decide to become nurses?"

"I love the uniform," Rosa said demurely, looking like one of Raphael's angels.

"Because Rosa wanted to be," explained Carol. "We have always done the same things."

"I said honestly," Roberta repeated. She knew the girls were clever and good students. They could be serious but not for long at a time.

"Believe me, we had a tough time getting permission from our parents," Rosa explained seriously. "I'm going to do public health."

"I'm going to be a doctor," Carol said defiantly. "And I dare anyone to stop me."

"More power to you, infants!" Roberta said heartily.

All at once graduation was only two days off.

Roberta was glad. She was very tired. It had been an extremely difficult spring. Even now the hospital har-⸗ored seven post-flu cases that bade fair to linger on for weeks. Yes, it would be good to be free again. She was going home for a long rest. The small colony at Shandleys was made up of delightful people and of course there was little Mary. After a rest she would decide just where she should settle. Already her list of prospects had narrowed to six or seven. Two were private, both staffed by doctors and nurses high in the profession. Perhaps there was no place for her in either establishment but she could at least send in her application.

Roberta had been in male surgical a week. She wondered how Rosa and Carol were getting on with Jackson, one of the general duty nurses who was quite devoid of humor. She hoped she wouldn't be too hard on the youngsters. Four o'clock. She left the table in the alcove and walked down the long ward. The eerie light of a wet June morning was creeping through drawn shades. Her practiced eye appraised each of the twenty patients. Already Mike Browning, legless now, was busy. In the few days she had been in the ward she had taught him to knit, and laboriously and still clumsily, he was thrusting the shining needles in and out of the colored yarn. He grinned as she approached and silently held up a curiously irregular block of bright wool for her inspection. It was to be an afghan

[63]

when the forty-eight blocks should be finished and added to it. Roberta examined it with interest and whispered:

"It's beautiful, Mr. Browning! You're doing famously," and continued on down the long room to the last bed where she slipped behind the screen for a glance at the old man who now lay breathing quietly, one gnarled, calloused hand relaxed on the white spread. His color was better. She felt the surge of thanksgiving she always experienced when an apparently hopeless case turned the corner and started on the road to recovery. It had been touch and go for nights on end but the old man clung tenaciously to life and it looked now as if the battle was won.

"He'll do," she told herself happily as she made a brief entry on his chart. "I'm glad the improvement came before I left."

She returned to the alcove. Myrtle Andrews had come up from Emergency to tell the big news she had known since early evening. Cynthia Cooper, on duty with Roberta, raised red-rimmed, heavy eyes, weary, yet still eager for any chance tid-bit of news.

"Oh, go take a nap somewhere," Myrtle told her as Roberta asked what was up. "You look like the end of a hard winter."

"That so?" Cynthia muttered, dropping her head on the table. "I can do it right here. Go on with your secrets. I won't listen."

Myrtle wrinkled her nose at the bowed head and said softly: " Gosh, Bob, I've been accepted! "

" You have? Grand! Now what do you have to do? "

" Just go to Buffalo for a physical examination, about six weeks' instruction and so on. The examination's all superficial—just a lot of red tape. I'm fit as a fiddle. Oh, Bobby, I can scarcely wait. While you're slaving in some hospital for a lot of selfish, unappreciative patients, give a thought to me—flying through the air with the greatest of ease." She hummed softly and did a little fandango.

" Superficial nothing," came Cynthia's muffled voice. " They go over you with a magnifying glass and a fine tooth comb. If you had indigestion last year from eating over-ripe clams they'll know it. If you ever had dandruff or an ingrown toenail you may as well hit the trail for home. If your heart belongs to some misguided male they'll turn you down. Superficial indeed! It's an examination to leave you nuder than when you came into the world—a physical test to end all—all hope of a job in that line. You're welcome to it. My cousin tried for a job on EAST-WEST AIRWAYS. She's not been the same since. Poor kid! "

" I hope you enjoyed your nap," Myrtle said snootily. " And I'm not your cousin."

" I'll say you're not," the other answered, her face still hidden. " She's a knockout. I guess that was the real reason they turned her down—she was too good-looking. You won't fail on that score," she said quite without malice. "Don't let me interrupt your confidences, gals—now that your hair's down."

"Oh, shut up!" muttered Myrtle. Roberta laughed. The two were always sparring yet were the best of friends.

"Don't mind her," she said. "She went on a picnic yesterday and hasn't had any sleep. Sure you'll pass with flying colors, Myrt. It's a grand life if you can get away with it." She spoke wistfully for she had thought of it for her own career. Beth and Neil, however, had raised so many objections she had given it up.

"I'm going to take flying lessons, too, Bob," Myrtle whispered, finger on lip. An exaggerated snore came from Cynthia and Myrtle went close to her and hissed: "Snooper, snake in the grass, faker!" Then a little louder: "Longworth!" and giggled as the other's head came up with a jerk. "Well, see you at breakfast, darlings." She grinned at Cynthia's scowling face and hurried away.

"Bet a dollar she doesn't make it," Cynthia said as Myrtle disappeared. "What I said was every word true—or practically so. Those babies are tough and Andrews isn't as strong as she wants people to believe. This spring hasn't helped her any, either. Are you willing to take my bet, Cameron?"

"Of course not," Roberta replied. "What makes you think she won't pass? Myrt's thinner than she was last

[66]

year but that doesn't mean anything—most of us have lost weight during this past six months. If there was anything wrong with her Gummerson would have discovered it. He's very thorough."

"Let it ride," the other said indifferently. "She may get by but I hope she doesn't. I don't relish any of my friends in that job." She yawned widely. "I wish I was getting through this morning. When I think of even two more nights of this I think I'll go nuts. Honestly, Cameron, don't you sometimes wonder why you ever decided to become a nurse?"

"Uh-uh," Roberta shook her head. "I always knew I should be a nurse. I wouldn't be anything else. I love it—most times."

"You would!" Cynthia said disgustedly. "You're the type! Oh, I suppose I'll stick it out. I'll work at it until something in pantaloons offers me a job raising his brats and darning his socks. It's a man's world, Cameron, and it's the woman who pays and pays for his reserved seat in the theater we call life." She sighed lustily. "The whole scheme's rotten, Bobby!"

"You *are* in a bad way," Roberta laughed. "My grandmother would have prescribed a stiff dose of camomile tea. Probably your liver's out of kilter from all the stuff you ate at that picnic yesterday. Better see Gummerson or go on a diet for a few days."

"You ain't got no sentiment," grumbled Cynthia pressing a hand to her tired head.

[67]

Lights began to glow in the panel beside the door and both girls got to their feet. The ward—the whole hospital was coming to life and nurses on duty were at once busy with washbasins, toothbrushes and last minute chart entries. Relief came at seven.

Cynthia's breakfast consisted of orange juice but Roberta was hungry and relished her toast, poached eggs and glass of milk.

Myrtle fell into step as they went down the hall to the corridor connecting the annex with the main floor of the hospital.

"Darn that Cyn, she's given me cold feet," Myrtle complained.

"It's just because she's afraid you will pass," Roberta told her. "She's worried something will happen to you. She confessed she hates planes. Imagine Cooper being nervous!"

"Well, I'm not and if I can't be a hostess I'll be a pilot. I'm crazy about flying."

"You're lucky to be able to gratify your desires, Myrt," Roberta told her. "Most of us can't."

While Roberta persisted in her assertions she was glad to leave the hospital—to have a vacation and be on her own—a registered nurse, she experienced a feeling of deep sadness as she said good-bye to classmates and faculty. She liked every girl in the class and was extremely fond of four or five. Now the chances were that never again would they all be together. She thought of the confabs in their rooms in the annex. Of their intimate talks and confessions. She remembered all the kindnesses shown her and regretted she hadn't done more in return. But the graduation exercises brought friends and relatives to the hospital and the excitement and gayety of the reception and dance that followed helped dissipate the gloom.

Will and Beth made a hit with Roberta's friends especially after they had extended a cordial invitation to Shandleys, whether singly or *en masse*. But they were eager to get back and, because of haste, Roberta was spared the pain of extended farewells.

As Will turned east at Faber Corners, Roberta recalled vividly following this same road months before. Tonight the air was soft, the lake molten silver in the moonlight. Will's big car purred along with never a protest but Roberta hoped the garage would have Jeremiah in good shape when she went for it next week. Somehow she and the old car belonged together. What memories! She grinned to herself in the dark. Just an old softy, that's what she was.

The Palmer house was dark; but it bore all the marks of being lived in. Awnings were at the windows above window boxes. Chairs were placed at intervals in the walled-in side yard. Roberta saw the gate was shut. She looked back as the car sped past and recalled that just a few months ago she had been a make-believe bride, entertaining guests in that very house. She wondered if Chris Baxter ever thought of that night.

It was after two o'clock when Will drove into his own garage at Shandleys. There was Prunella peering from the back door, her white apron the only discernible thing about her. A light went on in the kitchen and Roberta knew there would be a snack ready when they reached the house.

"I told her not to wait up for us," Beth complained as they went up the flower-bordered walk. "Honestly, Will, it doesn't do one bit of good for me to talk to her. She just does exactly as she pleases."

Will laughed. "Oh, why do you bother trying to discipline her, darling? You would get along much better and with less strain on your nerves if you would accept Prunella for what she is—a mammy as well as cook. She adores us all and her greatest happiness is in serving us."

"But she's old, Will," Beth protested. "I hate having her work so hard and—and——"

"She may be old but she doesn't show it," her husband said as they entered the brightly lighted kitchen and saw Prunella at the range, lifting fluffy scrambled eggs and strips of crisp bacon to a platter. She turned as the screen door opened.

"Nice time o' night to be gettin' home I mus' say, Mis' Beth. Won't be wuth nothin' in th' mawnin'. Yo' jes' stay right in bed an' get yo' some sleep. Sit down an' eat while things is hot. Nice time o' night to be gettin' home."

"Such a feast, Prunella!" Will exclaimed, drawing out his wife's chair. "You spoil us."

"Nice time o' night to be gettin' home," the old woman repeated, but the belligerence was gone from her voice.

"Why did you wait up for us after I told you not to?" Beth demanded in spite of a warning look from her husband.

"'Cause Mist' Will ain' never went to bed hungry yet an' I reckon he ain' goin' to 's long 's I's 'round, Mis' Beth. Hesh up, now, an' eat."

"You're an old fraud, Prunella Jenkins," Roberta laughed. "You know your curiosity wouldn't let you go to bed until we got home."

"Cur'os'ty kill' a cat mebbe; but I ain' dead yet, Miss Rob. 'Tain' no cur'os'ty kep' me on my feet when decent folks ought to be in bed. It's jes' plain dooty—I knows my dooty an' I does it."

"Was Mary good, Prunella?" Will asked, to change the subject.

"Good ain' no name fer what that chile am, Mist' Will. She an angel. They ain' one peep outta her sence yo' lef'. I set right there 'side her 'til jes' one minute ago an' she ain' move once. She th' spittin' image o' yo', Mist' Will."

"Like fun she is," Roberta teased. "Mary looks like me—everyone says so."

"Lookin' ain' bein', Miss Rob," the old woman insisted.

"She's only teasing, Prunella," Will told her. He leaned back from the table. "I feel heaps better. Now suppose we all march off to bed. No need for anyone to get up early tomorrow, either. It's Saturday and I'm playing hooky. That was a grand feed, Prunella." He laid an affectionate arm across her broad shoulders. "You're an old honey; but take yourself off to bed this minute."

"I'll jes' rense these here dishes——"

"You'll do nothing of the sort," Will said. He turned the switch and plunged the kitchen in darkness, then propelled the old negress to the door of her room which opened off it. "Good night, Mammy. Remember not to set your alarm."

"Alarm!" the old woman muttered in disgust. "I ain' never yit had to be waked up by no clock an' I reckon I ain' goin' begin now. Go 'long with yo', Mist' Will. I rises when th' spirit moves. G'night, Mist' Will—sleep tight, honey."

Will Macklin was smiling as he mounted the stairs. The threatened use of an alarm clock was an old joke between them. He yawned as his fingers automatically wound his watch. Roberta called a good night from her room. What a joy to sleep the clock around!

Chapter 7

Lazy days followed and Roberta was beginning to get bored with idleness. Shandleys Beach seemed even quieter than usual this summer. Beth said most of the young people were gone—married or vacationing else-where. The few who were left were either much too young or had definite interests of their own. Of course there was Mary; but Mary was still too infantile to respond to many overtures. Roberta decided she would get her applications off at once. She was sure life would become much more interesting if she knew definitely she had a job waiting.

She had never liked uncertainty and now she felt at loose ends. Even if she should not be expected to report for duty until fall, there was real satisfaction in know-ing just where she was going. She felt sure her vacation would prove much more enjoyable if her future were settled.

Roberta's keenest enjoyment this summer was in her

morning swim. She rose early, having enlisted Prunella's help. Promptly at 5:30 the old woman marched into her room, pulled the Venetian blinds with a clatter, then took a stand at the foot of the bed where she proceeded to deliver a speech on the evils of lying abed after sunrise.

Yawning and stretching, Roberta would drag herself from bed and into her swimming suit. By that time she was usually wide awake. She would snatch her robe, slip her feet into beach clogs and run down to the shore. It was seldom anyone joined her. Shandleys Beach folk slept late.

She swam out to the float one morning in early July, filled with energy and the joy of living. She had definitely decided to write the two private hospitals on her list this very day. Why wait? She was entirely rested and daily growing more eager to get back to work. The little she could find to do about the house took scarcely any time at all. Prunella, who resented the least implication that she was getting old, refused her help in everything except canning or making jelly. She seemed to enjoy assistance then. Beth was wrapped up in the baby and Will was just now working on an important case.

She closed her eyes for a moment. How heavenly it was to have the float—the whole lake—to herself! She sang softly, relaxed and happy. Her thoughts turned to Myrtle. Had she passed her physical test? She was to have taken it within a week or two after graduation; but of course those things took time. She had heard it was almost impossible to get a job as hostess on any of the lines and especially difficult to land one with EAST-WEST AIRWAYS.

Gulls dipped and swooped above the intensely blue water of the lake. It would be marvelous to be up there among the great fleecy clouds moving so lazily across the sky. Myrtle would make a splendid hostess. Pretty, clever and possessed of a lovely disposition, she seemed built for the job. Personality-plus, that was Myrt.

"Mind if I come aboard?" a voice from the other side of the float asked.

Roberta sat up abruptly. The smooth black head and broad shoulders showing above the water looked attractive and the smiling eyes met hers in bold friendliness.

"You look so completely at peace with the world I couldn't resist the temptation to get something more than a fish-eye view. I hope I am not intruding."

"Of course not," Roberta said, smiling in turn. "This is really public property, that is, to Colonists," she qualified.

"I wonder if that includes me. I'm staying at the Inn." He pulled himself up and sat down, cross-legged, beside her. "My name is Nichols—Stanley Nichols," he explained. "Doctor Nichols, to be explicit, though I'm still somewhat damp behind the ears."

"My R.N. is new to me, too, Doctor Nichols," Roberta smiled. "I'm spending my vacation with my sister over there on the Point. I'm Roberta Cameron."

"A nurse! That's fine. We ought to see a lot of each other." His black eyes paid tribute to her fresh young beauty. "You must have been here some time judging from the million dollar tan you have acquired."

"Since the middle of June—three weeks. I love it here. It's quiet and I know nearly everyone in the place. No one gets sick and my only night duty is the Saturday evening dance at the Inn and an occasional bridge game—nothing very late. It's delightful—for a while. I shouldn't like it for a steady diet." Her blue-gray gaze followed a swooping gull until it disappeared round the Point.

"I take it you enjoy your work. Well, so do I, but it's good to run away for a week or two—occasionally. I intend forgetting business during this vacation. I'm going to be the traditional playboy. I hope I can count on you to co-operate."

Roberta brought her gaze back to him. "Grand!" she said.

He might be fun. She had never cared, especially, for doctors; perhaps because during training she had been so closely associated with them. If this man wanted to forget he was a doctor, she was quite willing he should. He was very good-looking; Latin in coloring; tall, athletic, with clear-cut, regular features and slender, well-kept hands. Doctor but not a surgeon, was her decision after a glance at his hands. She told herself he was almost too handsome. She had always distrusted handsome men. Now the man's eyes met hers, a quizzical light in their velvety depths.

"Well," he smiled, "do I pass? Am I to be accepted as your number one playfellow, or am I presumptuous or—or trespassing on your hospitality?"

"I'm sorry," the girl said quickly. "Of course not. To tell the truth, I was fast becoming bored; had about decided to go back to work. That's what comes of familiarity, I suppose. Knowing the place and the inhabitants too well. Truly, Doctor Nichols, I'm afraid you will find it very dull here."

His dark eyes searched her face for a moment before he said with enthusiasm:

"Fine! I shall enjoy being dull—if it means all this." His arm made a sweeping gesture, taking in the attractive cottages, their gardens glowing with bright colored flowers, the wide expanse of placid water, the sailboats anchored near the Yacht Club a short mile away, and dropped again to his side. "Beautiful!" he breathed, his eyes on the vivid face beside him.

"It is lovely," Roberta agreed. The man's smile was a bit skeptical of her apparent complete lack of coquetry.

After that, the conversation was desultory. The early morning sun was only pleasantly warm. The gentle movement of the float acted as a sedative—making for easy friendliness and precluding active curiosity.

"There's an island off there in the distance that intrigues me," the man said lazily, pointing to a plume of smoke rising above a small forest of trees. "Do you know if it is private property or is one free to visit it?"

"It's private property but that doesn't mean we can't go over," Roberta replied, her eyes on the smoke that curled upward to melt imperceptibly into nothingness. "I know the people who own it. The Cuthberts are old friends of my sister. A man and his wife who come here summers, she to paint and he to work on his book. I'm sure you will enjoy knowing them. I'll call and tell them we'll be over and bring our lunch—if you like. They will adore that. Neva Cuthbert hates cooking and Joe never knows it's mealtime until food is set before him. They're an unconventional pair and great favorites with everyone."

"They sound interesting." He was pleased with her prompt acceptance of him. "About ten shall we say? We'll use the motorboat belonging to the Inn. Mine host told me it was for hire."

"I strongly advise against it," Roberta said. "It's far too temperamental. Let's take Arabella—I mean if Will hasn't loaned her for the day. He's quite apt to. There's my signal. Prunella waving a towel. See?" She stood up; pulled a white rubber cap over her bronze curls and returned the salute. "I'll be at the

[78]

Inn dock at ten or let you know," she promised and slid soundlessly into the water.

Stanley Nichols watched her long effortless strokes shoreward. The girl was beautiful and, what was infinitely better, appeared quite unimpressed by the fact. Slightly above medium height with firm, well-rounded body, wavy bronzy-brown hair and radiant vitality. He wagered her outlook upon life and the world through those heavily lashed, frank gray eyes was wholesome and sane—expecting the best of people and generally receiving it. So she was a nurse? He liked nurses. He had met some charming ones during his years of interneship. He had found them an intelligent lot as a rule, demanding from him nothing more than he was willing to give. Still, he had met none to compare with this lovely Roberta Cameron. She was in a class by herself—definitely. He looked down his slim, muscular length and smiled with satisfaction. He was glad he was six feet tall and that his legs were straight. Swimming trunks showed them to advantage.

His determination to get away from everyone he knew for a few days might prove not such a bad thing after all. He had experienced some difficulty in declining the rather urgent invitation to vacation at the Bartlett palatial summer home in the Catskills. Sylvia was no doubt hurt and bewildered by his refusal; but he had suddenly felt stifled—fed up with conditions. No knowing when the chance to get away would come again. He was glad he had stuck to his resolution. Roberta Cameron would be worth knowing or he had lost his ability to judge women.

During the days that followed, Roberta lived in an exciting new world. At first she fought against the almost breathless eagerness with which she greeted each new day. Beth teased her about her "crush" on the new man. Roberta wasn't given to crushes. Will, more soberly, wanted to know if she knew anything about him. Dependable, homely Will distrusted handsome strangers even as she, herself, had—until Stanley Nichols appeared.

"Why," Roberta said, eyes sparkling, cheeks rosy, "he's a doctor!"

"So what?" Will asked. Then derisively: "Aren't you the lady who protested her extreme loathing of doctors—men in general—but especially and quite definitely, doctors? But, seriously, Bob, do you know anything about him, personally?"

"No-o. But why should I?" Roberta demanded, chin up defensively. "After all, he's on vacation and so am I and he's good fun. Honestly, Will, to hear you talk one would think I was still a schoolgirl."

"Excuse it, please," Will muttered and subsided.

"That's all right, darling," Roberta said amiably, hastening to remove any trace of sting her quick retort might have given. "But really, Stan's a peach. I'm having more fun this summer than I've had in ages.

[80]

Don't worry about me, old dear. I can take care of myself."

"I hope so," her brother-in-law said softly, but Roberta didn't hear.

"Why don't you like him, Will?" Beth asked after Roberta had left. "Is it just the big brother attitude—the idea that no man is quite good enough for her? I should be jealous, darling, but I love your solicitude. I'm sure Neil, himself, couldn't be sweeter or more protective than you are. But you must remember that Bobby is twenty-one—nearer twenty-two. I was married—to you, remember, a perfect stranger to the family—when I was barely nineteen. And I hadn't Bob's training or her independent spirit."

"Granted," her husband conceded. "But then, remember, my dear, it was I whom you married—not some handsome man from God-knows-where."

Beth laughed. "You're funny, Will. But listen to this. Neva Cuthbert told me Jim feels just the same as you do about Doctor Nichols and we agreed it's just plain jealousy. Neither you nor Jim could pose for America's handsomest man although we'll concede you're the two best—no, dear, I'm serious, and you just naturally distrust good looks in a member of your sex. Isn't it being a little unfair to him to turn thumbs down because of something he can't help?"

"It isn't his looks altogether, Beth," Will persisted, "and Jim agrees. It's something else. I suspect Nichols is what one calls a women's man—ladies' man I think the term is. I bet when he starts practicing, his clientele will be 99 per cent female. Want to bet with me?"

"Oh, you men!" Beth scoffed.

Chapter 8

ROBERTA WASN'T SURE JUST WHEN SHE KNEW SHE WAS in love with Stanley Nichols. Perhaps it was the afternoon they were caught in a storm off Cobb's Point ten miles up the lake from Shandleys. Of course this was the day Arabella chose to indulge in one of her rare fits of temperament and quit cold. Stanley rowed in to shore and they found shelter in a shack until the storm was over. During those hours of intimacy, when rain pelted on the roof and wind whipped the lake to a white fury, the two talked of many things and were amazed to find they had so much in common.

After the storm, came the long row home, Roberta taking her turn at the oars. Perhaps it was the way Stan looked into her eyes as he steadied her into the boat, or maybe it was the way he said: "Good girl!" when she eased Arabella into the slip beside the Macklin dock. She knew only that her heart raced and her pulses pounded as he took her arm and hurried her through the drenched, low-drooping flowers bordering the path to the cottage.

"Better get into dry clothes at once," he urged solicitously. "That's what I shall do. See you later, Berta."

She watched him leap the low hedge and sprint down the drive. And she who had always boasted of her independence and ability to fend for herself, found it sweet to be taken care of. She went upstairs, took a hot bath and changed into fresh clothes, all the time in a happy dream.

Perhaps that was only the beginning. Maybe it was at the Inn dance the following night, when she saw him talking to Clarice Stark. Clarice was a blonde with an air, confident of the value of her dimples. Roberta knew a jealous pang as she watched them. Suddenly Stanley turned; their eyes met and he came to her. Her spirits soared.

But there was no doubt about it the day she brought the little Burtless boy to shore after he had gone down twice. She had persisted in her efforts to revive him minutes after those nearby insisted it was useless. Stanley arrived just as Teddy's lashes fluttered, and took over.

"He'll do now—thanks to you, Berta," he said after a moment.

Roberta swayed to her feet. He caught her as the world went black before her eyes. She was in her own room when consciousness returned; Beth and Will standing anxiously near; Stanley's fingers on her pulse.

Yes, she was sure that was when she knew she loved him and he loved her. His eyes were eloquent. She had closed her own, blinded by the flame of that look.

But he didn't tell her he loved her until the day he received the summons to return to New York. He was going in with Jason Massy, the heart specialist. Roberta had known his vacation was nearing its close but so was her own—she hoped. She intended working right up to within a week of her marriage. She wanted to be a true helpmate to her husband. A doctor needed an efficient and understanding wife. She would be that kind. She wished Stan was going in for general practice. Maybe he would later. She fancied he needed money rather badly. She didn't like the idea of his specializing. The world was so much in need of competent general practitioners—like old Doctor Compton, their family physician for three generations and still an authority on pediatrics.

An early morning thunderstorm had delayed their swim. Now at nine o'clock, the air was clear and sweet. Raindrops still clung to the flowers bordering the garden walk. They had reached the porch. Roberta suddenly felt guilty. She had not been listening to Stan's enthusiastic recital of Doctor Massy's phenomenal success. Of his interest in a small private hospital—

devoted exclusively to the care of wealthy women whose most common ailment was too much leisure.

"Isn't it a break for me?" he asked. "I have been hoping against hope—keeping my fingers crossed all this past fortnight. Now my future is assured. Let's make a day of it, Berta. Let's celebrate."

"Oh, I'm sorry, Stan, but I can't go far from the cottage today," Roberta told him ruefully. "Beth and Will have gone to Bramton and I promised to look after Mary. And besides, I'll be tied up practically all morning with Prunella. However, this afternoon while Mary is napping, we could go down to the beach—our own beach. I shall be in sight of the house and yet we won't be disturbed."

He looked disappointed and reluctant to accept conditions. Roberta had considered his reasonableness about small, irksome things one of Stan's most endearing traits. Now, however, he frowned.

"It's so seldom I see you alone, Berta," he complained. "Either Beth or Will or someone is always butting in. Even Prunella does her share. One would almost think there was a conspiracy to keep us apart. Even when we go right away, I have the feeling someone is quite apt to pop out and spoil our trip. But with Will and Beth away, maybe I can have you to myself for a little while. How about three or half-past? Will the baby allow of my coming then? I—there is something I must tell you."

Roberta was confident she knew what it was. This afternoon he would ask her to be his wife. A sudden shyness overcame her. After all, she had known him scarcely two weeks. How was it she was willing to give her life into his keeping? Oh, she was glad she was young and healthy; glad she had beauty and was a nurse. Stanley would be proud of her and she would devote herself to the glorious task of making and keeping him happy.

"Just why are you busy all morning? Surely Prunella is competent." His voice seemed to come to her from a long way off. She forced herself to speak calmly, to still her inner trembling.

"Believe it or not, Doctor Nichols, I am canning berries and making jelly," she said. "You see, the fruit came and Beth had already promised Will to go with him. Prunella, who is positively the best cook in the world, refuses to tackle the job alone so I offered my expert services."

The frown on Stanley's face deepened. "So you put jelly making ahead of me—my pleasure and on my last day, too," he chided. "Not very flattering. Somehow I had an idea I rated higher than that."

"Don't be silly," the girl laughed. "That has nothing to do with it. I didn't know you were counting on this particular morning. I can't let all that fruit spoil."

"Of course you can't." His tone was ironic and Roberta was troubled. Then she smiled. He was like a small boy who suddenly discovers he can't always have his own way.

"Of course I can't," she repeated. "One must be thrifty and I assure you I make very good jelly. You shall have a sample this very day. Come early and we'll have a long afternoon right at the end of the garden. It's shady and we can have tea out there and maybe a swim before dinner. Beth and Will will be back early. Don't look so abused, you silly boy. You're not leaving today."

"Tomorrow morning, and I don't think you care a damn whether I leave or not. You're cold, Berta. *You must can fruit!*"

"But I do care, Stan," Roberta assured him.

He caught her hands in his. "Do you? Tell me you mean it—that you love me," he urged, his fine eyes pleading; his eager hands drawing her nearer.

Roberta lifted a glowing face and he crushed her in his arms. Time stood still. How long they remained in that close embrace neither could have told. Suddenly a screen door slammed. Prunella shouted as if all in the house were deaf:

"Here they am, Miss Rob. What'll I do now?"

Roberta drew back from Stanley's arms. "I'll have to run," she whispered, a caressing hand on his cheek, "but you'll come back early, darling, won't you?"

Stanley Nichols kissed her again and left just as Prunella poked her head into the hall to see why

Roberta didn't answer. She gazed at the flushed face with wise, disapproving eyes.

"I knows somebody whut's got kissed pretty thorough," she said to the kitchen in general. "Best not let Mist' Will see yo' lookin' like yo' jes' read yo' title clear to mansions in th' skies. He ain' takin' no stock in that there Nichols doctor."

"Oh, Will!" scoffed Roberta. "Will thinks I'm still a child. He's jealous of every man who looks twice at me. Anyone would think I was Mary instead of merely his sister-in-law."

"Mist' Will put a sight o' store by yo', Miss Rob. Don' yo' ever fergit that. Thinkin' o' marryin' this here doctor, Miss Rob?"

"He hasn't asked me, Prunella," she replied with the careless certainty that of course he would.

Prunella shook her head. "H'mm. Kisses ain' meanin' nothin' 'less they's 'comp'nied by a' invite to see th' preacher," she said wisely. "Some men got th' idee they's conferrin' a favor on a gal when they kisses her. Sort o' make her feel good. Miss Rob, don't yo' take no stock in jes' kisses. Wait 'til yo' shore his 'tentions am hon'able an' he means bizness 'fore yo' wear yo' heart on yo' sleeve an' yo' love in yo' eyes. I knows whut I's a-talkin' 'bout. Yo' lissen to me, Miss Rob."

The advice reached Roberta vaguely as in a dream. She still felt the pressure of Stan's lips against her

[89]

own. Two weeks and he had made no attempt to kiss her although she had, more than once, felt he wanted to. She had held aloof. She wanted to be sure. And now she was sure—so blessedly sure!

"What did you say, Prunella?" she asked, when the old servant's silence made her aware she had, as usual, been bestowing advice.

"Nem min', Miss Rob," Prunella grunted. "A gal in yo' condition ain' takin' nothin' from nobody. It's like castin' pearls 'fo' swine as th' preacher says—only yo' ain' swine, 'zak'ly."

Roberta laughed. "Thanks," she said. "Let's get on with the canning before Mary wakes. Here, I'll take care of the fruit while you get the jars ready. It ought not to take long."

"Tak' long's need be, I reckon," the old woman muttered, "an' it'll be a murricle if it 'mounts to beans—way things am."

"Stop muttering, Prunella, and get those jars ready," Roberta ordered, "and after lunch when Mary is in her play pen, we'll plan dinner. Doctor Nichols will be here for dinner tonight, so set a place for him. I'll telephone the market for broilers, Prunella, and we'll have peas, too."

"Mis' Beth goin' have th' res' o' yes'dy's roas' fer dinnah tonight, Miss Rob. She tole me jes' whut she want an' that's whut we goin' have, too." Prunella was stubborn and Roberta tried to coax her into changing the menu. The old woman wouldn't budge. "I wuk fer Mist' Will an' Mis' Beth an' I does whut Mis' Beth say. We goin' have cole roas' beef an' salad fer dinnah an' hot mushroom soup to start an' if that Nichols doctor don' like it he can go back to th' hotel an' eat there."

"Why don't you like Doctor Nichols, Prunella?" Roberta asked though she thought she knew. Will didn't like Stan, for some reason, and what Will thought was gospel to Prunella who took him from his dying mother's arms, brought him up and worshiped the ground he walked on.

"I ain' a-sayin' I likes him an' I ain' a-sayin' I doesn't like him," Prunella said grimly. "But he ain' goin' git no broilers when Mis' Beth say roas' beef. No ma'am!"

That settled it and Roberta sighed. It wasn't like Prunella to object to pleasing her. No, it was just because Will had some fantastic notion that because Stan happened to be a stranger and good-looking, he must necessarily be untrustworthy. However, she didn't care. Stan was a darling and she loved him. As for dinner tonight, Stan might even prefer taking her out to dine and dance. They had gone to Maple Grove on several occasions where the food was really excellent and the orchestra superlative.

"Oh, I don't care," she said airily. "We'll probably not stay home anyway. There are lots of grand places to eat around here. Places where they serve broilers, too, Prunella," she added, hoping to touch the woman's pride.

"Umph!" was all Prunella offered and the two worked for some time in silence.

At last the fruit was finished and Mary was in her pen near the side door where Roberta could watch her. She was a good baby and seldom made any fuss. Bathed and fed by three o'clock she was back in her crib on the sleeping porch upstairs, and Roberta, carefully dressed, went out to the little hedged-in garden to keep her tryst.

Prunella brought a chair to the garden side of the back porch and rocked. She was sewing on a garment of scarlet sateen and it made a brilliant splotch of color against the white siding of the cottage. Every little while the protesting rocker gave a lurch and Prunella would gasp: "O-oh, Lawd!" then settle down again to a steady swaying. Roberta endured it as long as she could.

"Why don't you go around to the shady side of the house, Prunella?" she called.

"'Cause I prefers to stay right where I is," the old woman replied shortly.

"Then, for Pete's sake, stop rocking."

Prunella's chair became painfully still. She sat like a monument—immovable. Roberta laughed ruefully. She got up and went down to the beach. Mary always slept until four or half-past and if she should cry, Prunella would go to her.

She settled herself on a bench beside the boathouse and gazed with dream-filled eyes over the quiet lake. A red canoe shot out from the Cuthbert pier. Probably Neva going after the mail. She wondered just why Joe Cuthbert wasn't particularly cordial to Stan when they stopped at the island from time to time. Joe had always encouraged her to bring her friends so he could give them "the once over" as he called it. Day before yesterday she had felt that Neva, too, appeared less friendly to him—failing to respond to Stan's amiable overtures. Maybe Stan hadn't noticed; but she supposed her love made her sensitive—perhaps over-sensitive. She wanted her friends to like him.

Miles away, a train whistled as it approached Bramton. A plane came into view and her eyes followed its flight across the lake until it vanished into the hazy distance. Complete happiness enfolded her like a garment and she sighed in ecstasy. How quiet it was—the mid-afternoon stillness of a hot July day. Too warm for bathing, the beach was deserted except for a few small boys some distance away.

Her heart caught as she watched Stanley come through the garden in search of her. Prunella was no longer in sight and Roberta wondered if she had gone upstairs, from which vantage point the beach was in full view. Well, she didn't care.

As he drew near, Stanley stretched wide his arms and she ran to meet him. In his close embrace she forgot her irritation at Prunella. In fact, she forgot everything. Nothing mattered but his arms about her and his lips on hers. He drew her to the bench beside the boathouse and they sat down, close together, her hands in his, her head against his breast. A complete and perfect silence fell—words were no longer necessary. She could feel the heavy beating of his heart against her cheek and knew that her own kept pace with it. Occasionally he murmured some endearment against her hair and she closed her eyes, shyly reluctant to let him see her complete surrender.

"I wish I didn't have to leave tomorrow, sweetheart," he whispered at last. "But I'll try to get up again—in a few weeks. You're so sweet, Berta!" His voice sent little waves of ecstasy through her whole body.

"I never expected to marry a doctor, Stan," she said dreamily after a moment. "The girls at the hospital always laughed at me because I used to swear I loathed doctors." She laughed softly. "I told Will the same thing a few months ago, and now look at me. But I'm glad I took that training, Stan. I want to be an understanding wife. I want to help you with your practice all I can."

Was it her imagination or did his arm grow suddenly lax? And why was he so silent? She stirred uneasily. With a smothered imprecation his arms crushed her. His kiss was fiercely possessive.

"Darling," he whispered hoarsely, "you know I love you, don't you?"

"Why, of course, Stan," Roberta said, gray eyes raised to his in surprise at the question. "I *should* know. I love you, too."

"Then help me, now."

"Help you? What is it, dear? Tell me." A little stab of dismay widened her eyes and unconsciously she shivered.

Chapter 9

IT ISN'T A PRETTY STORY, BERTA," STANLEY NICHOLS
began, the arms about Roberta relaxing. "You see, I
was born on the wrong side of town." The low voice
became suddenly bitter. "My people were desperately
poor. Oh, it wasn't genteel poverty. It was mean, miser-
able, wretched want. My mother died when I was just
a kid—I don't remember her—I don't want to. My
father deserted me. I was brought up somehow—by the
neighbors—derelicts like myself."

"It doesn't matter, darling," Roberta comforted. "It
isn't your family, it's you I love."

He continued as if she had not spoken. He appeared enthralled—swept along by the story he was
telling. "When I went to school, I had to pass the
Bartlett estate. A girl lived there, a lovely, frail child,
motherless but with the richest father in town—also
the most visionary. His old aunt who lived with him
was as bad or worse. The little girl, Sylvia, used to

watch for me and we became friends. Soon she invited me in and I met her father and the aunt. After that, we played together every afternoon when school was out. She taught me tennis and dancing the way she had learned. I was an apt pupil, I suppose, because I wanted to amount to something and knew this was the way. In return I taught her to swim effortlessly, like a fish; to build a fire and to follow a trail in true Scout fashion. Oh yes, the Sunday School got me into a Scout Troop. Missionary work," he muttered.

Roberta pressed his hand sympathetically. How splendid that he had come so far—and by his own efforts!

"One day Sylvia decided she wouldn't attend the exclusive day school any longer. She would go to public school with me. Her father thought well of me. He said he envied me my ambition. That was a laugh. It seems he had always lacked initiative. He told me poverty was the greatest goad to success. I didn't tell him it was the curse of mankind—the slayer of souls as well as of bodies. I didn't tell him because young as I was I had already learned the art of listening wide-eyed to the platitudes of the great, the near-great and the wealthy. So Sylvia and I walked to and from school together. It wasn't far from her home and when on stormy days the chauffeur drove her—he drove me, too. I thought, sometimes, he hated the job—of driving me, I mean. He was a dour sort of chap—a great believer in caste. I was quite beyond the pale. We entered high school together, Sylvia and I.

"Somewhere I had picked up the idea I wanted to become a doctor. I thought I could work my way through college and medical school. I was just a simple young fool with ideas of grandeur, never realizing the gigantic task I had set myself. I was graduated from High School and won a scholarship. Mr. Bartlett gave me a fountain pen and his aunt and Sylvia a gold wrist watch."

He shoved back his coat sleeve. The watch was beautiful. Roberta had admired it before.

"You see, Aunt Sylvia approved of me, too. She admired ambition—in others. Sylvia went to college." He paused for a moment. "Her father died suddenly in her freshman year. His death made Sylvia a very rich girl. She was then eighteen—my own age.

"Somehow, I managed to get through that first college year. I shall never quite know how I did it. The following summer I worked at the camp in the Catskills, mostly as a playmate for its young mistress. The Bartletts call it a camp. It's a mansion in the midst of acres of forest and lake. It was that summer Sylvia and I went on a long tramp through the woods. We both loved hiking and went farther than we intended. Suddenly, in some way, I caught my foot and plunged down a ten foot embankment fracturing my right leg. Sylvia had always been a frail girl. Her heart had never been strong but the doctors felt outdoor life was helping her materially. Between us we improvised a rude stretcher and Sylvia dragged me along the trail to the nearest camp—miles of rough going, then collapsed."

The pause was eloquent. Intensely interested though she was, Roberta fought down the feeling that this was an oft-repeated story—that Stanley was overdramatizing everything in order to win sympathy and applause. She was instantly ashamed and caressed his cheek with tender fingers. The low tense voice went on:

"I realize I was a blind, selfish fool. I ought to have known she shouldn't have done it; but I was in pain and thoughts of infection and possible amputation scared the common sense out of me. All I could think about—all I could see ahead was my blasted career.

"After that experience, Sylvia was very ill for a long time. She had strained the muscles of her heart beyond repair so that afterward only the very mildest forms of exercise were allowed her. She didn't return to college. I shall never forget the agony and shame I experienced during my enforced invalidism. And although neither Aunt Sylvia nor the girl herself blamed me in the least—I blamed myself. Then, too, the situation wasn't made any easier for me by the outspoken criticism of certain other relatives who considered me more or less of a chiseler.

"Sylvia was sweet, Berta. I had always thought of her as a sort of sister but somehow after that we drifted into an engagement. She insisted upon paying my college tuition and, later, financing my medical training. We have been engaged ever since and were to have been married this fall as soon as I became definitely established. I insisted upon waiting until then."

Roberta had drawn away from his encircling arms and now sat in frozen silence. Stanley got to his feet and strode up and down the white path, his handsome head bowed in an agony of rebellion.

"I'll pay her back—I swear I will," he said, pausing before her. "Help me, darling. Tell me what I should do. I don't love Sylvia as I love you." He sank to his knees beside her and clasped her hands tightly to his breast. "Won't I hurt her more by marrying her, loving you, than if I explain it all to her now? Oh, Berta, I'm a heel! How can you possibly care for me? But you do—say you do, sweetheart!" he pleaded.

Roberta looked into the face so near her own and a spasm of revolt—of self-pity shook her. Why should this be her lot? This Sylvia had everything—had always had it—wealth, social position, every advantage, while she had nothing—only Stan's love. Why give him up? He was leaving the decision to her. He wanted her advice. Why throw away their happiness because Sylvia had bought Stan's allegiance? Bought it with money she didn't need. After all they had only one life to live and everyone had a right to happiness— to fight for it if necessary. And she was a more fitting wife for Stan than this sickly, no doubt utterly spoiled Sylvia Bartlett. A doctor needed a strong wife, an understanding and helpful one.

She closed her eyes. Unbidden came the vision of that slim, delicate girl risking her life so that the boy she loved might have prompt medical aid. Somehow Roberta knew Sylvia loved Stan—had loved him from her childhood. She knew she had given her love unselfishly—lavishly, just as she gave her money so this boy from the wrong side of town might realize his ambition.

Her head lifted. The fine sensitive conscience bequeathed her by a long line of Scotch Presbyterian ancestors shrank from a happiness obtained at such cost. No. Stanley Nichols belonged to Sylvia Bartlett. Stan must save his honor and Roberta Cameron preserve her integrity. She withdrew her hands from his and rose to her feet.

"Of course you must marry her, Stan," she told him and marveled at the cool steadiness of her voice. "There is no question about it. You owe it to her—that much, at least." She swallowed with difficulty and went on: "We must forget this brief madness. It ought not to be hard. We have our work and—and—you must never let her know."

She tore herself from his restraining hands and ran toward the cottage praying that Beth and Will would not return until she had recovered somewhat from the effects of the shock she had received. She must never see Stanley again—never. She couldn't stand it.

She had barely reached her room, however, when Will and Beth drove into the yard. She got up and locked her door and, face down on her bed, fought, dry-eyed, the hardest battle of her life—a battle against complete despair. Beth knocked and asked if she were ill; but Roberta couldn't answer. After a moment she heard Beth go away. She hoped they would leave her alone. She tried to reason with herself—tried to believe it was nothing more than disappointment or, at worst, hurt pride. After all, two weeks ago she had not known Stanley Nichols existed. Why should she feel as if happiness, life itself were completely over? It was wrong. It must be. She would not let it get the better of her. She would conquer this terrible gnawing ache—this hopelessness. "The way to conquer a difficulty is to face it; a battle faced is half won." It was almost as if her father had spoken. She sat up.

Stanley Nichols was leaving in the morning. She must not see him. She would go away at once. She had planned on spending a day or two with Virginia Southard, Neil's fiancée, in Pan's Haven. Now was a fine time to do it. She slipped down the hall to the bathroom and dashed cold water on her face—pressing it against her hot cheeks and aching eyes. Beth called from the foot of the stairs:

"Is anything the matter, Bob? Are you ill?"

"Of course not," Roberta replied and was dismayed that her voice sounded thick and strange. Just as she feared, Beth ran up the stairs and burst in upon her, sympathetic but eager to know what had happened.

"What is it, Bob? Why are you staying up here? Did something happen? Tell me." She put her arm about her taller sister and stared into the stricken face.

"Oh, it's nothing, Beth. Only—only—I've sent Stan away. He—oh, don't talk about it, please. I'm going over to stay with Ginny for a while, but don't tell him—anyone where I am."

"You sent him away, Bobby? But why, if you—if you care for him? Don't mind what anyone says if you love him ——"

Roberta broke away and went into her own room where she tossed clothes into a suitcase and snapped it shut. Beth, who had followed, eyed her wonderingly.

"Is there anything we can do, darling?" she asked.

"Not a thing. It was all a mistake—I have acted like a silly child, Beth. I guess Will is right—I'm naïve—take people at face value—believe anything—take chances—foolish ones." Why was she saying all this? The words tumbled out without her volition, it seemed. "Tell him for me, I'll never do it again. Tell him I have grown up at last. He need never worry about me any more. Good-bye, Beth. I'll be back—in—a day or two."

She ran down the stairs and out through the side

door to the garage. Beth caught Will's arm as he prepared to follow.

"Leave her alone, darling," Beth said. "She's better by herself just now."

"But where's she going in such a hurry?" he asked.

Beth was at the telephone calling Virginia Southard.

"Bob's on the way over, Ginny," she said, "and for heaven's sake don't ask her any questions. No, I hope it's not terribly serious—but she's been hurt—just act as if nothing has happened and—keep her for a day or two if you can. Okay, Ginny. Be seeing you soon."

Prunella announced dinner just as Roberta backed Jeremiah out of the garage, turned and roared away. Will shook his head. Prunella's black eyes rolled.

"I see whut comin', Mist' Will," she said darkly. "He likely got a wife an' chillun, all we knows. I tole her an' I tole her, Mist' Will, an' she won' lissen. We knowed he ain' no man fo' her, Mist' Will."

"He? What he? I don't know anything, Prunella," he said. "But if you mean the handsome doctor who's been cluttering up her vacation, I'd like to spoil that classic face of his with a good healthy punch. What's he done to Bob?"

"Um-um!" Prunella muttered darkly. "Wouldn't I, jus'! I'll put a spell on 'im, Mist' Will. That'll learn 'im not to fool 'roun' innercent young gals."

"Hush, Prunella," Beth commanded crisply. "Neither you nor Will knows a single thing against

Doctor Nichols. He is a gentleman, certainly, and just because he is handsome doesn't make him a villain, Will Macklin. No doubt Bobby has her own particular reasons for refusing to marry him. Of course she refused him." Beth stared at her husband with eyes defying him to contradict. Prunella set the platter of " cole roas' beef " on the table with a thump. She eyed her Mist' Will doubtfully for a moment and that young man gave her a reassuring nod.

" Glory be! " the old woman cried. " Oh Lawd— hallelujah! He deliver da lam' outa de lion' mouf— praise His holy name! Amen! " and fled to the kitchen.

" Honestly, Will," Beth sputtered indignantly, " sometimes that woman exasperates me almost beyond endurance."

" Ca'm yourself, honey," her husband soothed. " You know darned well you'd be absolutely lost without Prunella, bless her heart! "

" Oh, you! Well, anyway I happen to know Bobby refused to marry Doctor Nichols and you needn't act as if she didn't. There was some good reason why she wouldn't consent to be his wife. I don't know what it is; but I do know she quite definitely told him ' no.' And don't you ever think otherwise, Will Macklin. I know my sister."

" I wonder," Will murmured.

" What do you mean by that? " Beth demanded indignantly. " She is absolutely frank and open in everything she does. There is nothing mysterious about Bobby."

"And like a child in her knowledge of the ways of men. She expects the best from people—sometimes she gets it. With all that hospital training when she must have knocked up against life in the raw, she still refuses to see anything but good in her fellow humans. A girl like that is bound to get hurt. I only hope I'll be around when she needs help."

"You're another Jeremiah," his wife scoffed. "Maybe she named her old wreck after you instead of the prophet. Roberta's young and lovely and some day the right man will come along and she'll be happy and make him happy. You'll see, you old pessimist!"

But Will had seen Roberta's eyes as she flew past him and when next morning Doctor Nichols called to bid them good-bye, Will experienced keen satisfaction as he noted the chagrin in the young man's face when he learned Roberta had gone on a visit leaving no message for him.

Chapter 10

ROBERTA DROVE THE SIXTY MILES TO PAN'S HAVEN IN A
daze. She had no awareness of the country through
which she passed or whether or not she broke traffic
rules. She seemed to be driven by a force outside herself. She had to get away. Virginia Southard saw her
guest's perturbation and, thanks to Beth's warning,
refrained from making any comment. Roberta was
grateful. She desired no one's pity. All she wanted was
to be left alone.

The summer settlement of Pan's Haven browsed
beside the river. The cabins of rough logs and native
field stone were separated each from its not too near
neighbor by nothing more than a rugged trail. No
attempt had been made at landscape gardening; the
owners being entirely satisfied to let Nature have her
way. The result was delightfully restful. No golf within
five miles and no tennis nearer than the village. Two
sizable bathhouses at the man-made " swimmin' hole "

were the only concessions to civilization. The business and professional men who owned cabins in Pan's Haven seemed content to fish, swim and hike and loaf—mostly loaf. Once in a while a more strenuous soul would suggest a game of quoits or hand-ball on the beach. For social activities, the inhabitants piled into cars and drove to Bramton, Corinth or even farther, to Syracuse. But this was not often.

Not many young people were content to remain for the entire summer; it was much too dull; but Virginia loved it, for with Neil perhaps in danger on the other side of the Atlantic, she had no desire to mingle with her gay young contemporaries.

Quiet, beautiful and completely unspoiled, Pan's Haven was just the place for Roberta to get hold of herself—to face squarely whatever the sunless future promised. Her throat ached, her eyes burned from emotions controlled too long. She sat on the lower step of the cabin porch and listened to the voices of the night. The moonlight outlined the trees in silver. The soft wind sang a love song to the leaves. Birds murmured sleepily in their nests. Occasionally an owl hooted, its lonesome cry finding an echo in her heart. She didn't look up when Virginia dropped down beside her and laid an affectionate hand on her knee.

"Decided just where you're going to settle, Bob?" she asked softly after a moment in which she scanned the unhappy face of the girl beside her.

Roberta shook her head. "I haven't heard. I sent an application to the hospital in Garsden."

"Garsden? Oh, to the Rebecca Moore Memorial. I know something about that place. Doctor Theron Holmes is Chief of Staff. He's a wonderful surgeon, Bob. I hope they take you on. That's where Mother went the time she fell and injured her back. No one else could have done what Doctor Holmes did. You'll love working with him, Bobby."

Roberta didn't appear to hear. Her wide gray eyes were on the river, dappled with moonlight, moving unhurried and soundless to the lake miles below—eventually to the sea. The exhaust of a speed boat shattered the stillness and she sighed in relief when the alien sound died away. A canoe holding two half-naked paddlers slipped silently by, hugging the shore, their glistening bodies in bold relief. Across the river a huge bonfire was lighted; strains of a dance orchestra drifted in on a pine-scented breeze. Tears slid down her cheeks and she made no effort to wipe them away.

"It's all so lovely here," she said at last. "So lovely, it—it hurts."

"I know," Virginia murmured. "It is lovely." Then more briskly: "And how we sleep up here! Honestly, sometimes I can't even remember getting into bed. I'm asleep almost as soon as I shut my door. Tomorrow we're going to have a steak roast over at the Ledge. Dad's coming up early and will bring the steaks. I wish we weren't going to be the only young people there, Bob. Do you mind?"

"Mind?" Roberta cried, almost violently. "I'm glad of it."

Mrs. Southard joined them and they fell again into silence. Roberta felt that silence pour over her—flooding her bruised heart—soothing her bitter questioning —quieting her rebellious soul. The jovial voice of Mr. Southard calling good night to a neighbor was like a blow. She winced. She was in no mood for conversation. Mr. Southard always teased her and tonight she couldn't endure it. A feeling of shame brought her to her feet. It would be terrible if she, always so companionable and free from silly sentimentality, should suddenly burst into tears like any undisciplined adolescent.

"Mind if I turn in early, Mrs. Southard? I'm—I'm terribly tired." To her dismay her voice broke and her hostess hastened to assure her it was quite all right if she went to bed at once. Virginia didn't make any move to accompany her and it was only later that Roberta realized her thoughtfulness and understanding.

"I'm not going to be a sap," she told hereslf fiercely as she undressed in the tiny guest room. "I shall not go about advertising myself as a crushed, broken creature demanding sympathy. This is something that was bound to happen. It is just what Will has repeatedly warned me against. I'm too simple—I imagine people are exactly what they seem. I took it for granted that because Stan said he loved me, he, of course, expected to marry me. I—I even told him as much. I thought I could read all the signs. And oh, the road of life isn't that easy! Why, even Prunella has more sense than I."

Suddenly she flung herself across the narrow bed and allowed her bitterness to have full sway. When the storm had subsided she felt weak and shaken but somehow cleansed of bitterness. She could still hear the low murmur of voices on the front porch and slipped down the narrow hall to the tiny bathroom where she plunged her face into cold water, then went silently back to her room and to bed. She lay for a moment with closed eyes and lax body listening to the sighing of the wind in the trees, and, suddenly, the sun was streaming into her room. Eight o'clock and the appetizing odors of coffee and broiling ham made her reach for robe and mules and sent her posthaste to the kitchen. Virginia was making fresh coffee.

"Lazy bones!" she chided. "I've been for a swim already. If you go this minute you can have your dip and be back before Mother gets up. Dad left an hour ago. Skip along, the water's grand."

Several people, strangers to her, were already in the pool and Roberta didn't linger. She was surprised to find she was hungry. Only last night she had wondered if she could ever eat again. She discovered, too, that the morning was glorious. She hurried up the trail toward breakfast with a feeling almost of guilt that she dared be glad she was alive and hungry.

During the morning she and Virginia paddled up the river to the village. Roberta felt proud of herself— she was acting very sensibly and really it wasn't nearly so difficult as she had thought it would be. Somehow, Stan seemed very far away this morning, and the tragedy of her unhappy love something out of the distant past.

Was it possible it was more hurt pride than anything else? For the first time she found herself criticizing Stan for daring to make love to her while he was bound to Sylvia. But perhaps he couldn't help it any more than she could help loving him. She closed her eyes and saw again his pleading face begging her to help him. To do what? To betray the girl who had given him so much? Not likely. There could be no permanent happiness for either of them that way. She was glad she had sent him back to Sylvia. Her head went up in proud defiance, then she looked down at her hands and found them clenched so tightly about the paddle her fingers ached. She made a wry face at Virginia's unconscious back.

"Sa-ay!" Virginia cried, "not so strenuous. Slow and easy does it, my girl."

Roberta laughed ruefully. "I haven't done much paddling lately, Ginny."

"Oh, you Sybarite!" the other chided. "You miss half the joy of a vacation by clinging so to civilization."

"Try to convert Beth," Roberta suggested, "especially since Mary appeared."

"Mary's a darling," Virginia agreed. "I'd even forego all this, and I love it, for a baby just like her. Don't you think she's like Neil, Bob?"

"I think she's like me," Roberta declared. "Everyone does except Prunella who swears she's the 'spittin' image' of 'Mist' Will,' which of course is plain libel. Will's a lamb but he's certainly no Robert Taylor."

"Well, you and Neil are alike," Ginny insisted.

"Sure we are," Roberta agreed.

At the village post office, Virginia found a letter from Neil and the two girls pored over the closely written sheets of thin gray paper, shuddering over the dangers they felt sure he was encountering and laughing at the droll stories he told. If Roberta felt a pang of envy at the other's happiness, she hid it carefully. She determined to go back to Shandleys Beach and let them see she was not at all broken-hearted; not really the simpleton she had appeared when she rushed away so tragically yesterday afternoon. She would tell Will he need not worry about her ever again for she was now thoroughly sophisticated. She had no intention of letting him blame Stan. It was just one of those things entirely beyond their control. "An act of God," Chris Baxter would no doubt have called it. She wondered if he had come to feel that way about his own broken romance. Well, one thing was certain, Chris Baxter would never let a disappointment ruin his life and neither would Roberta Cameron. Such mistakes were seldom, if ever, fatal to the ultimate happiness and success of either participant.

So, despite urgings to stay, Roberta drove back to Shandleys Beach that afternoon. Beth breathed a sigh of relief when she saw her and Prunella bustled about the kitchen, humming the mournful tune that invariably presaged something extra special for dinner. Tonight it would be "Miss Rob's" favorite shortcake. When Will drove into the yard, Roberta went to the garage to meet him.

"Now don't say 'I told you so,' my dear brother," she said slipping her arm through his. "The whole thing was just one of those silly blunders that sometimes occur even in the best regulated families and we'll all forget it."

Will turned her round and eyed the unnaturally quiet face raised to his; examined the blue-gray eyes and slightly pensive mouth. "Do you mean—you don't mean—then you are going to marry——"

Roberta's somewhat tremulous laugh interrupted. "Of course not. I said it was all a blunder, didn't I? Doctor Nichols is a splendid man. He happens to be engaged to another girl. I hope he will be happy—that they will both be happy."

Will said nothing for a moment, then with unexpected suddenness he swore roundly and with so much deliberate vigor that Roberta went off into a paroxysm of hysterical laughter. Will, who was such a stickler for decency both in morals and manners! He patted her on the back, his face a thundercloud, then he, too, began to laugh.

"A tempest in a teapot. Thank God that's over," he said and hurried her to the house.

Two days later, Roberta packed her bags and left Shandleys Beach for Garsden. Rebecca Moore Memorial Hospital had accepted her application and wished her to report for duty immediately. Roberta was glad. In spite of her brave front, she felt the need of work—exacting, fatiguing labor that would completely fill her heart and mind; that would leave no room for idle longing or weakening regrets. An unhappy chapter was ended. She would not let it darken her future nor in any way influence her outlook on life. One couldn't regulate love. Stan's was much the harder rôle; but she must not let her sympathy for him undermine her determination to forget him.

Chapter 11

WHEN THE TAXI DEPOSITED ROBERTA'S LUGGAGE ON THE porch of the nurses' home in Garsden that warm July afternoon, two familiar arms drew her close.

"I heard you were coming, Cameron," Cynthia Cooper cried. "Morrison asked me about you when I was in her office. I did my darnedest to give you a black eye but the fact you were one of my classmates was all the recommendation needed. What a rep old Weston has! Gosh, Bobby, I'm glad you're here! Seems like old times." She rattled on while she led the way upstairs and helped Roberta unpack.

"It's grand seeing you, Cyn. I had no idea you were coming here. Like it?"

"It could be worse." Cynthia was always conservative in her praise, fearing possible future disappointment. "Holmes is an old crab but he knows his stuff all right. He's a wiz with a scalpel. The joint's 'way out of date, though. What's really needed is a swell big fire and a million dollars for rebuilding. Morrison isn't half bad—sort of motherly and 'loathes this slovenly habit of addressing nurses by their last names.' Quite different from Longworth over in Weston. The girls are okay as far as I can see; but the internes are—you know—nuts."

"What happened to that swell private case you had mapped out for yourself? Mrs.—Mrs.—Curtis, wasn't it?" Roberta asked.

"Oh, they hustled her off to a sanatorium. I didn't even get one single crack at the job. But as long as you are here, I'm glad I didn't get it. I felt sort of stranded, somehow. Life here is very different from Weston. I guess all private institutions are different. I know they aren't nearly so strict. Morrison believes in the honor system for the staff and another thing, all the nurses are graduates. There is no training school here. That makes it easier for us, I think. Although sometimes it might be convenient to have a probie or student to lay the blame on. Nothing doing though. If we make a mistake or slip up—why, we lose some privilege for a time. Not many do, though. Sometimes I think it's the rule itself that inspires violation. The very fact that Weston banned all social intercourse with doctors and internes endowed them with glamor and heaven knows none of them ever had any. We found that out quick enough when we smashed the rules to go out with them. While Morrison isn't keen about it here, still it is left to our discretion and sense of fitness. One or two of the consulting staff aren't half bad and Lewis, the resident, is a lamb; but wait till you meet the pair of internes we are harboring at present. Webster's a nut and Taney's a case of suspended development, though we all like him. Ready? I'll show you around."

Roberta's first job was in Receiving and she was glad. The excitement incident to the work there did a great deal toward restoring her sense of well-being. Life moved fast. Incidents happened, grave and gay. Responsibilities were met and a tragedy occurred that touched and left its mark upon her life. But that, she knew, was living. Comedy, drama, tragedy—she experienced them all. She discovered Cynthia was right in her appraisal of the two internes. They were the oddest pair she had ever encountered, but in entirely different ways.

Summer passed. September was warm. Nurses straggled back from vacations and the hospital settled down to normal conditions once more.

Doctor Webster had become something of a nuisance to Roberta. He persisted in his attentions in spite of her marked indifference. The other nurses found the situation amusing and Roberta tried not to let them see her resentment. Then, one day, out of a clear sky, he asked her to marry him. Roberta was too astonished to do more than stare at him in speechless consternation.

"Look, Cameron," he said, "I want you to go to India—oh, not as a missionary—just for research work. There'll be some medical—surgical—hospital work of course, and honestly I think you'd make a swell assistant. I know you don't care especially for men—you have shown it all too plainly. It would have to be marriage, I suppose, but we might make it merely a business arrangement. We could really do grand work together. What say?"

"You're out of your mind, Doctor," Roberta replied coldly, "or else you're joking." She looked up at him with obvious distaste.

"Oh, I'm quite sane, I assure you." He planted himself squarely before her in the basement corridor. "And I was never more serious in my life. Will you consider it? It really isn't as impossible as it sounds. I admire you more than any woman I ever knew; what is more, I respect you."

"Thanks for those few kind words," Roberta said, unable to keep the sarcasm out of her voice, "but I assure you I have no intention of marrying anyone— ever, and I certainly haven't the least desire to go to India. And please, Doctor Webster, don't ever refer to this again. I don't like it—not one bit. Will you kindly let me pass?"

The young man flushed. An angry light dawned in his small blue eyes. "There is nothing in my proposal to enrage you, Miss Cameron," he muttered. "I'm

[119]

offering you an honorable name and a chance to do some worth-while work in the world and you——"

"Hello, pals!" a rollicking voice interrupted. "What goes on here? Fade away, Webby—you're bothering the help." Doctor Taney snapped his fingers at his disappearing colleague and turned a quizzical gaze to Roberta who was having difficulty in controlling her anger. "I bet he's been offering you his honorable name and a share of his Gladstone bag." He lifted a restraining hand to stop Roberta's indignant protest. "Don't tell me—I want to guess. Quote: 'I admire you more than any girl I have ever known and what is more important, I respect your ability.' Unquote. Right? Don't take him too seriously, Cameron. The chap's wacky. Oh, no. He's clever enough, in fact, he's nuts about bugs but he wants a nurse with him when he goes to India."

"But why pick on me?" Roberta asked in distaste.

"Oh, you're new here. There have been others before you in his plans for the future, my poor darling. You were kinder to him than some of the others. Usually the girl leads him on just to make a monkey of him. Don't let it bother you."

"Thanks for the information, Doctor Taney," Roberta said loftily. "He doesn't bother me in the least. How did he happen to come here if——"

"His father and the Chief were buddies in the world unpleasantness of 1914–1918 and he thought association with Doc might be good for the lad. I'll say this for Webby, he knows his stuff. The old man's fond of bugs, too. You ought to see 'em in Lewis' lab. Mad as hatters, both of 'em."

"But Doctor Holmes is a surgeon. I didn't know ——"

"That he is also a scientist? My child, surgery is his vocation—bugs his avocation. Mine, too, but in somewhat milder degree. So don't let Webster get in your hair. He's harmless—just wacky."

"I wish he would transfer his affections to someone else."

"He will. Aw, here I go."

The loud speaker summoned him to bring in an apparently dying man from over on the East Side. Roberta returned to Receiving which had been empty and quiet now for more than an hour. She busied herself with the filing system she had inaugurated, while her assistant finished cleaning up Emergency after the last patient now resting quietly in a cool private room on the third floor.

Betty Scott came into the outer room, her face damp from perspiration. She brushed back an unruly curl of blond hair, then removed her cap in order to pin it more firmly in place. She applied powder to her nose and used a lipstick carefully.

"Weather like this makes me wish I had kept my boyish bob," she said, adjusting her cap before the tiny mirror above a cabinet. " I'm going over to the kitchen for ginger ale. Want some?"

" If it's cold when it arrives," Roberta said. " If you're not coming right back with it, don't bother."

Betty laughed. "Depends on the dirt they spill over there how long I stay," she said as she departed.

Roberta thought the diet kitchen must have proven especially interesting because Betty lingered. The ambulance returned bringing in an old man. Doctor Taney took him to Emergency and helped him to the bed.

" Cardiac asthma, Cameron," he told her as he came out. " He's not in a particularly dangerous condition though. Fix him up and the resident will be along directly. Better call him, nurse. Gosh, but it's a scorcher today!"

Roberta got the patient ready for his physical examination and put in a call for the resident. The telephone operator began the monotonous paging of Doctor Lewis.

Minutes passed. " I'm trying to get him," Margaret insisted when Roberta urged haste.

" Well, keep on till you do," Roberta said. " He's needed here at once. If you can't get him, try for Doctor Taney. He must be here somewhere. But get someone."

She heard the labored breathing of the old man and hurried back to him. On her way she grabbed a tank of oxygen and a mask. His face was a dark bluish gray. She administered oxygen but it didn't help—he seemed too far gone. Why didn't someone come? She felt sure nothing but morphine would quiet those terrible bronchial spasms but she was fully aware she had no right to give a narcotic or any drug without an order. What to do! The man was undoubtedly dying. He had to have help and at once. Job or no job she must do something. It was criminal to wait longer. She drew a slow quieting breath then calmly and deliberately prepared the dose and gave the hypodermic injection. The response was gratifying. Both she and the patient breathed easier.

"How goes every little thing, Cameron?" a breezy voice asked and the owner strolled nonchalantly into the room.

"Haywire," Roberta retorted succinctly. "What did you mean he was in no particular danger? The man nearly died and Margaret has been paging Lewis for ages."

"Lewis is over in delivery—triplets," the young man said. "Why didn't Maggie call me?"

"She did. Why didn't you come? Over in the nursery, I suppose—inspecting said triplets. Now listen. I had to give him morphine. Oh, you needn't look so disapproving. I saved your hide as well as the poor fellow's life. Get busy and write an order."

"Tut, tut, child, and if I refuse, what then?"

"Nothing, I suppose, to you. I shall undoubtedly lose my job and possibly my license as well, and you know it; but of course that will be my funeral, not yours." Roberta spoke indignantly. "It's the first time I ever did such a thing—the first time it was ever necessary. What sort of a hospital is this that the staff ignores summons just because it's hot or a child is born—in triplicate? Maybe I didn't do so well coming here, after all."

"Say not so, darling," the young man begged. "Say not so. You are an ornament to any establishment. Your charming presence in this dump makes even me willing to finish my year." Roberta had turned away. "Aw, don't be mad, Cameron," he soothed. "It's nurses, God-bless-'em! it's nurses who are responsible for ninety-nine and forty-four one hundredth percent of the hospital recoveries. And like morticians, they cover up our mistakes. Long may they rave! Sure, little treasure, I'll sign that order. I'd sign anything for you—even a marriage license."

Roberta stamped her foot in exasperation. "Honestly, Doctor Taney," she exclaimed, "I don't know how they put up with you here. You are the most irritating, aggravating——"

"Popular and likable chap in the place. I know it, darling—I know my worth but modesty forbids my making a public statement to the effect." He wrote the order for morphine and signed it with a flourish.

"There you are, my saucy wench, and what do I get for it?"

"I know what you ought to get," Roberta told him, but she was smiling. "What sort of a doctor do you expect to make?" she asked, filing the order.

"I'm going in, almost wholly, for pediatrics, darling. Kids adore me and I get a big kick out of them—especially when I can help them back to health."

"I know," Roberta said, somewhat abashed at her anger. "I suspect your clownishness is a pose——"

"Sure it is. If I didn't clown I'd break right down and bawl my heart out at your cruel treatment of me." He grinned wickedly.

"Oh, get out of here," the girl cried. "You're a pest!"

"And you're just about the loveliest gal in the world, Roberta Cameron," he said softly. "And if my heart wasn't hopelessly entangled already, I swear I'd wear down your persistent opposition to male attention and carry you off to my two-rooms-and-kitchenette for life."

"Then I'm glad you're engaged, Doctor Taney, for two-rooms-and-kitchenette couldn't hold me. I demand a wider sphere of action. Who's the girl, Doctor? A nurse?" Roberta was herself again.

"Uh-uh," he shook his head emphatically. "No nurses for me! I loathe the creatures—snippy, stuck-up, opinionated upstarts. Who do they think they are, taking affairs into their own hands and browbeating and subduing males into doing their bidding? There ought to be a law —— School-teacher. The girl next door. We grew up together and I proposed to her the first time I ever saw her. I was four and she, a young lady of three weeks, was being displayed by her proud mama. I'd like you to meet her, Cameron. You'd love her."

"I'm sure I should," Roberta agreed. "And I wish you all the luck in the world."

It was that night she received word Myrtle Andrews had passed her test and would make her first trip on the third of October. Roberta wired congratulations. In the next mail she received one of Myrtle's pictures in the uniform of an E-W Airways Hostess. Myrt stood beside a plane, lips smiling, hand raised in gay salute. Roberta placed it on her dressing table and there was an immediate rush among the nurses for application blanks. It was quite useless to tell them the chances of their getting a position was practically nil. Tall and short, thin and overweight, plain and pretty, they all wanted to take the chance.

Followed thrilling letters from Myrtle. She had acquired her pilot's license. She was supremely happy. After a time she wrote of a certain pilot—one Jim Preston who had been wonderful to her. At Christmas, Roberta received an ecstatic letter announcing her engagement to him. At Easter—tragedy! The plane Jim Preston piloted and in which Myrtle Andrews was hostess crashed just east of Denver and all nine passengers and crew were killed.

"Oh, Bobby," wept Cynthia, face downward on Roberta's bed. "I knew something like this would happen. I had a premonition—I tried in every way possible to prevent her taking that job."

"I know. But it is what she wanted to do, Cyn. I wanted to do it, too. Even now I wouldn't be afraid. We all have to die and if we die doing the thing we love it must be a happy way to go. And at the last, Myrt had the joy of being with the man she loved. That's something. I have an idea she was never the least bit afraid even if she knew a crash was inevitable. I can imagine her quieting the others, if there was time, and smiling encouragement to the very last."

"But what a waste! Myrt was a swell nurse. Everyone loved her and—oh, Bobby, she was too young to die!"

"Listen to me, Cynthia Cooper," Roberta said quietly. "By dying young she may have missed a lot of misery and suffering. No one knows what the future holds for him—if he did perhaps he would prefer death to living on. I think none of us has the right to say death comes too soon when we don't know from what death may be saving us."

"But death is so final—so complete, Bobby!" wailed Cynthia.

"I heard someone say it is only stepping through a

door into another room, Cyn." Roberta's voice was low, her eyes dreamy. "You see, I have a mother and father in that other room, darling, and I want to see them again. Now Myrtle is there, too."

Cynthia's sobs had ceased. She sat up. "Gosh, Bob!" she said curiously, "you sound as if you'd got religion!"

Roberta smiled. "I have, Cyn. I've always had it."

"Oh, I know that," the other retorted. "I meant the real thing, like the missionaries and the deaconesses and—well—the Salvation Army lassies. I'm a church member, too, but I—well—I'm not exactly on friendly terms with death."

"You should be by this time, Cynthia," Roberta said. "You certainly come in contact with it often enough."

"Yes, and I still fear and hate it. I fight it every inch of the way. I won't give in and I don't pull my punches and it's only because the big bully has been in the game longer than I have and knows more ways of weakening the patient's resistance, that I sometimes fail. It's always a blow to me, and I hate death worse than ever after every defeat."

"Granted," Roberta said, glad the other's wild grief was over for the present at least. "Ours is a work of healing—of hope; but I believe we live more fully, more healthily and happily by overcoming fear—all kinds of fear—even the fear of death. Surely you have felt relief when some soul slips away from a tortured or tired body in search of rest. Don't you know of any cases where death has been kind?"

"Oh, in the very old and the ones we are convinced are hopeless, perhaps, but even then I fight for them."

"Of course. We all do. That's our job and we fight because we don't know the answer. Oh, I suppose I can't make you understand just the way I feel, Cynthia," Roberta said. "And don't think for one moment that I am eager to die. I'm not, and if I'm ever very ill, I hope you will take care of me. I like your fighting spirit, darling. Count me on your side every time."

Chapter 12

REBECCA MOORE HOSPITAL WAS FULL OF RUMORS. THE late Senator Moore, grandson of its founder, had left most of his considerable estate to this memorial to his grandmother. The staff was jubilant. It meant a larger, more modern building, new equipment and an assistant surgeon—long considered but until now financially impossible. Miss Morrison, the middle-aged superintendent, went about with shining eyes and step as quick and elastic as that of her youngest nurse. New life seemed to have entered the staid old establishment and even the patients felt the change.

The hospital was not large—less than two hundred beds, but then Garsden was not a very large town. The main building was four stories high. The operating room on the top floor; the solarium on part of the roof. The maternity building joined the main hospital by a long unheated corridor. Contagion and pediatrics were each in a separate building as was also the nurses' home. Now, perhaps, the whole plant would be brought under one roof which would make things more convenient for patients and easier for the entire staff.

Doctor Taney left the hospital at the end of his year and Roberta received an announcement of his marriage to " the girl next door." Doctor Webster went to India but without his nurse. There were other changes. One or two weddings among the nurses and the confusion and excitement of the remodeling and refurnishing of the entire hospital, while continuing to serve the community, kept the staff busy. Doctor Holmes' dream slowly materialized. The hospital became one of the most beautiful and quite the most useful building in the county.

The days flew by. June, and Roberta went to Corinth for her brother's wedding. The war in Spain was over. Immediately after the ceremony, Neil and Virginia flew to San Francisco where they embarked for the Orient. The whole world was seething with unrest—Neil must be in the thick of it. Roberta spent her vacation in Maine, coming back refreshed and wearing a becoming golden tan. In November Doctor Holmes' wife died suddenly and the surgeon spent more and more time in the hospital. His scientific research began to create something of a stir and doctors came from far and near to attend his clinics. He wrote excellent articles for medical journals and was in demand at conventions. It became more and more apparent that the hospital must have an assistant and Doctor Holmes promised the Board to produce one all in good time. Being completely aware of the chief's ability and efficiency, the Board tabled the matter for another period of time.

Roberta had heard nothing even indirectly from Stanley Nichols since reading the announcement of his marriage some year and a half ago. Convinced she had forgotten him and sure her heart was quite whole again and intending to keep it so, life seemed to take on new meaning. She loved her work. The entire staff considered her outstanding. Miss Morrison depended on her and Doctor Holmes singled her out for special responsibility.

Cynthia Cooper fell precipitately in love with a young advertising salesman and after meeting his family settled down with remarkable patience to an indefinite period of wishful waiting. Roberta considered it a strange state of affairs. Cynthia waiting for any man! She decided love did queer, unaccountable things to a person.

In January rumor spread through the hospital by the grapevine route that a new doctor was coming to Garsden, but not the long expected assistant to Doctor Holmes. It was disclosed this new man was a nephew-in-law of the chief. Roberta had heard Doctor Holmes speak of a nephew and a niece, but was unaware the niece had married a doctor. This new doctor would be assistant to Doctor Wharton who, getting on in years, wanted a younger man at his side. The new doctor and his wife were to live in the Holmes mansion. Since the death of his wife, the surgeon had been lonely and then, too, he wanted to keep an eye on his niece who, it was reported, was somewhat of an invalid. No one seemed to know the newcomer's name and it was a distinct shock to Roberta when she came face to face with Stanley Nichols in the comparative privacy of the small unheated room where flowers were kept during the night. He caught her hands and swung her around to the light.

"Berta!" he exclaimed softly, thrillingly. "I knew you were here. Doc spoke of you at dinner last night. It seems you stand well with the old boy. I've been trying to get a chance at you alone, but have been tied up." His voice deepened. "Why did you run away from me?"

"Run away?" Roberta asked, dismayed and confused.

"Don't hedge, Berta," he said. "I walked the floor all that night and dashed over to your place first thing in the morning only to be told you had gone on a visit. Why did you do it? You knew I had to see you again."

"But there was no reason why you should," she reminded him.

[133]

"Ah, but there was. You see, I had decided not to take your advice—your cruel advice. Oh, it's heaven seeing you again. Now life will be bearable. You are a sight for tired eyes and lovelier than ever. If you only knew how I have hungered and thirsted for a glimpse——"

"Hush! Oh, please——" Roberta begged, her heart hammering. Her hand went out in a gesture of pleading and despair.

He went on as if she had not spoken, his words rushing along impetuously. "It has not been easy, Berta. When you ran out on me I was in despair. Then I endeavored to see things as you did and I tried, Lord, how I tried, to forget you. I've tried to make Sylvia happy. I hope I have. I even gave up my job with Massy to come here so her uncle could keep her under his eye. I'm glad, now, that I did. It's fate, Berta. Don't you see? Where can we talk? I must see you alone—away from the hospital."

Roberta was too bewildered to speak and was relieved when another nurse joined them. With some meaningless remark, Doctor Nichols left the room. Roberta busied herself with the flowers for her patient, her mind in a turmoil. She must leave the hospital at once. To go on seeing Stan day after day, perhaps working with him, listening to his voice, was too much to expect of any girl—no matter how complete the cure. She had been so sure she had recovered—that she no longer cared. Yet at his touch all her carefully built defenses went down. She felt defeated—helpless.

She lay awake that night planning some plausible excuse for leaving—some reason that would satisfy the chief without rousing suspicion. At last she decided she would merely announce she was making a change. After all, it was nobody's business why she would wish to leave Garsden.

Miss Morrison was upset. Seldom had she known a nurse so perfectly adaptable and thoroughly efficient. She was loath to release her and went directly to Doctor Holmes.

The surgeon sent for Roberta. He fired questions at her. Why was she leaving? Was it a matter of salary? But she had known when she came what salary to expect. Had something happened to influence her decision? He told her with blunt but flattering frankness that he hesitated to release her. The hospital had come to depend on her. Rebecca Moore was proud of its personnel and didn't welcome change. Wouldn't she reconsider? Perhaps a brief rest was indicated. It would have to be brief because as she knew every member of the staff was in demand. The hospital was full as always at this time of the year.

Roberta's spirits sank lower and lower during the interview. She felt depressed and ashamed for her seeming ungraciousness. She was sure Doctor Holmes had shown her consideration far beyond her merit and she knew he was annoyed and bewildered by her sudden action. Roberta thought:

"This is what comes of joining the staff of a private institution in a small town. People grow dependent upon—more strongly attached to their associates than in larger places."

Suddenly the surgeon's keen glance seemed to sharpen and he remarked with apparent irrelevance: "Doctor Nichols seemed pleased to find you on the staff."

Roberta's blood left her heart. She tried to control her suddenly shaking knees. "Face it—the best way to overcome a difficulty is to face it." Her mouth felt dry. She swallowed with difficulty and managed:

"That was kind of Doctor Nichols. You are all kind and I don't want you to think I am ungrateful, Doctor Holmes——" she began, but he silenced her with a motion of his hand.

"Think it over carefully, Cameron," he growled, "and I hope you will make up your mind to stay on with us. That is all."

It was Stanley who decided her. Stan who summoned her to Doctor Holmes' office that same evening.

"You can't leave, Berta," he said, his voice compelling. "Especially right now. Sylvia's uncle isn't any too fond of me as it is and from the way he spoke of your leaving just at this time, sounded as if he thought I was in some way responsible. It can't be that you are running away from me—again, Berta. That means you still care. Oh, my dear, you have no idea what it means to me knowing you are here—knowing I may see you every day—hear your voice, even touch your hand. Can't you understand that I need you? Cold as you are, you must know that I'm still mad about you. I was a fool ever to let you talk me into giving you up. But even your friendship can mean much. You are so strong, Berta. You put duty before love. Can't you see you're needed? The hospital needs you—the chief needs you—I need you."

He had struck the right chord. She was needed. She was strong—she could help him to be strong. The blue-gray eyes she raised to his were filled with pure devotion. He experienced a touch of chagrin. Was this devotion for him or for what he represented—the hospital? He caught her hand and pressed it against his cheek watching with satisfaction her expression change. The devotee became once more the sweetheart of that summer idyl.

Roberta drew her hand away and stepped back. "Very well." Her voice was low and uneven. She was shaken. Where was her vaunted strength? Where the integrity that had sent Stanley Nichols from her to another girl? The situation was even worse now because he was the husband of that other girl. He was absolutely nothing to her and never could be any-

[137]

thing. Her nerves steadied. "I will stay. Putting it that way, I suppose I have no alternative. But please remember, Doctor Nichols, the madness of summer before last is entirely over. I refuse to let you go on believing there is anything in my heart but friendship for you. You must believe that or I cannot remain here. Doctor Holmes has been wonderful to me. I admire and respect him."

Why did the picture of young Webster flash before her mind's eye—to bring an involuntary smile to her lips? She didn't want to smile. Doctor Nichols' frown lifted at that smile.

"Of course you do, Berta," he murmured. "Doc's a great surgeon in spite of his years. I am glad to be able to be of help to him—to lift some of the burden he has been carrying far too long. I don't care what your reason for remaining, so long as you stay. Good girl!"

The telephone rang and while he was answering, Roberta slipped from the room.

The weeks flew by. Doctor Nichols seemed to spend a great deal of time at the hospital. Roberta made a desperate effort to go on as if nothing had happened— as if her safe and sane little world had not suddenly become filled with hidden dangers and subtle temptations. She told herself repeatedly and emphatically that her love for Stanley Nichols was quite dead and for days at a time she would feel relieved and buoyantly free. Then would come an encounter with him in some secluded part of the hospital and he would catch her hands in his and once, before she could prevent it, he drew her into his arms. At his touch her defenses threatened to crumble, though they never quite did. But the encounter left her fearful that some day she might surrender, and she was bitterly ashamed of her potential weakness.

It was after one such encounter that she slipped into 127 where Cynthia Cooper was on duty. She felt she couldn't go back to Paula Winslow, the lovely but disagreeable young divorcée, just yet. She knew she would have little patience with her temperamental outbursts. Cynthia was always so stimulating and Roberta knew she was sadly in need of a stimulant of some kind.

Old Mrs. Benson, crocheting in a wheel chair by the window, smiled at her as she entered.

"Come in, my dear," she called hospitably. "See what I am making for my girl here. It's for her hope chest. Would you like me to make one for you? It's a luncheon set." She held up a block for inspection. "On my good days I work fast. Pretty, isn't it?"

Roberta examined the delicate cobweb and admired it as enthusiastically as Mrs. Benson could desire. Cynthia beamed. "I wanted to buy the thread for it but she insists when she gives a present she gives it all and with no assistance from the recipient."

"That's the only way to make a gift," the old lady insisted. "Do you want ecru, my dear, or white?"

"But I have no hope chest, Mrs. Benson," Roberta told her.

"You see?" Cynthia said. "Just as I told you, Mrs. B., the gal's impossible."

"I don't believe it," the invalid replied. "It's high time you started yours. Every girl has a hope chest, or maybe she calls it something else these modern days. But no matter, just so it is a part of her dowry." She spread the bit of lace on the blanket covering her knees. She looked so happy and proud of her handiwork that Roberta said impulsively:

"I shall love owning one, Mrs. Benson. You are sweet to suggest it."

Cynthia patted her arm. "Atta girl!" she whispered.

"Oh no. I'm not at all sweet, my dear. I'm a fussy old woman with more leisure and money than I can comfortably use. You girls have been thoughtful and good to me and the least I can do in return is to be pleasant—when the pain's not too bad—and make a bit of beauty for your future homes." Her bright eyes gazed intently at Roberta for a moment. "No girl as lovely as you will be allowed to remain single for long, my dear. My girl here tells me you are in danger of going through the woods in search of perfection only to pick up a crooked stick at the end of the trail." Her gaze grew reminiscent, her voice gentle and a little sad. "You see, my dear, much to the dismay of my friends, I picked the crooked stick at the very beginning

[140]

of the journey and it became my staff and comfort until just a little while ago. That is why I must depend on others—my crooked stick was taken from me. It was such a lovable crooked stick—we were so perfectly suited to each other." Her voice died away and the old eyes took on a far-away look.

Cynthia had slipped from the room. It was time for her patient's mid-morning milk.

"I'm sure you were," Roberta murmured. "And don't listen to Cynthia, Mrs. Benson. I just haven't time to go into the woods for any kind of stick—straight or crooked. But don't worry your dear head about me. I'm perfectly happy and quite sufficient unto myself. Now I must run or Mrs. Winslow will complain of neglect instead of surveillance."

"Pauline Carling should have been spanked thoroughly and systematically when she was small, my dear. Ada spoiled her. She never held with the Biblical instruction that to spare the rod is to spoil the child. Of course children differ; but I am sure Solomon had just such a child as Pauline in mind when he wrote that passage in Proverbs. The fine boy she married is happier without her. Run along and give her my love—for her poor father's sake. Between Pauline and her mother John Carling's path has been a thorny one."

Roberta went back to her patient. She didn't hurry. Mrs. Winslow had practically told her to get out—she wanted to be alone. The door was ajar and as Roberta entered the flower-filled room, she saw that Doctor Nichols was seated beside the bed, chatting with its vivacious occupant. Mrs. Winslow frowned as Roberta came in.

"Why don't you go take a walk—or something?" she asked bluntly. "It makes me nervous to have you constantly hovering about like a fussy old hen."

"Oh, that's not fair, Mrs. Winslow," Doctor Nichols rebuked, shaking a finger at the pouting girl. "I'm sure no one would ever accuse Cameron of hovering."

Paula Winslow laughed and caught the admonishing finger in her beautifully manicured hand. "Well, she's fussy, anyway. I hate being watched—and don't call me Mrs. Winslow—I like Paula much better."

Roberta turned away in disgust. She longed to tell her she had other things to do than watch her and that she wasn't any happier at being assigned to the job of nursing her than the capricious lady was in having her. Instead she murmured a meaningless: "I'm sorry," and slipped into the hall where she encountered Cynthia Cooper laden with a huge florist's box for Mrs. Winslow.

"These just came and Bennet asked me to bring them up. The gal sure drags 'em in, doesn't she? Is she receiving this early in the day?"

"Not exactly," Roberta said dryly. "Doctor Nichols is there."

"I'll warrant he is," Cynthia agreed cynically. "How

quickly that man scents a pretty face—and a fat bank roll!"

"Don't be catty, Cyn," Roberta reproved and wondered why she wasn't angry at the criticism. Was it because she was jealous of Paula Winslow? Jealous? What right had she to be jealous of anyone? "Perhaps she sent for him."

"I haven't a doubt but she did, Bob. Davis said she has had him in every evening since she's been here. Seems to have fallen hard for him. But then all the females in this hospital—in the town for that matter—between the ages of eight and eighty are making idiots of themselves over that jitney. Poor simps! It seems even the members of the Board—the female members—are becoming sex conscious."

Roberta laughed at her vehemence. "What did you call him?"

"Who? Nichols? Jitney—five cents. About his value in my estimation."

"I take it you don't admire the new doctor, then?" Cyn was funny with her snap judgments.

"Oh, I grant you he's handsome all right; but I never could assimilate oil, Bob, and Nichols reeks with it. He's too smooth. Of course it goes over big with a lot of subnormal women—they're his meat and he basks and purrs at their adoring approval. But I bet you he'd double-cross his own mother to get what he wants."

Remembering Stan's story of his childhood—his saying: "I don't remember my mother—I don't want to," Roberta thought it not unlikely and was instantly ashamed of her disloyalty.

A tinkling peal of laughter came through the half-open door and Doctor Nichols was smiling as he reached the hall. He ignored Cynthia's presence and stood for a moment until she had turned the corner.

"Don't take anything to heart that Paula Winslow may say, Berta," he advised. "We've just got to humor her. The girl's neurotic—too much night life—too much money and not enough to interest her. And remember, Berta, two of her aunts are on the Board—very influential ladies. So, just take it all in your stride. It will pay in the end."

"I don't mind in the least," Roberta assured him a trifle stiffly. "A nurse soon learns to take it." She attempted to pass but he caught her hand.

"Don't be like that, Berta," he whispered.

"Nurse!" called an imperious voice and for once Roberta was glad to hear it. Stan laughed softly and tiptoed away.

"To whom were you talking outside?" Mrs. Winslow demanded.

Roberta longed to tell her it was none of her business, but said coolly: "One of the nurses who brought you these flowers, Mrs. Winslow. And Mrs. Benson asked me to give you her love."

The girl laughed unpleasantly. "Old Lady Benson can keep her moth-eaten love. I certainly have no use for it. Give me the card—there, you've dropped it."

Roberta retrieved the card and gave it to her. The discontented mouth broke into a smile for a moment and she examined the flowers with critical eyes.

"How many times has he sent roses, Nurse?" she asked, holding the flowers at arm's length. "Aren't there any other flowers in this town except roses?"

Roberta counted the cards bearing the name Bertrand Payne. There were seven such cards but the first flowers had long since faded. She announced the fact to her patient and that lady said crossly:

"Put them in a vase just as far away from me as you can. Roses make me sneeze—especially his roses." She turned her back on the room and was silent while Roberta arranged the flowers and returned to her seat just outside the door to await further demands.

She wondered why Mrs. Winslow disliked her. It was a new experience and she longed for an explanation but knew none would be forthcoming from her. Perhaps it wasn't personal at all—merely aversion to nurses in general. Davis, however, said it was because Roberta was far more beautiful and Mrs. Winslow was jealous.

"She's nice as pie to me and I'm homely as mud," the girl laughed. "I could never be a rival, Cameron. Nichols doesn't know I'm alive. The other men who call concentrate on her. I'm just hospital atmosphere. I heard her tell one man not to call during the day. I saw through that maneuver even though she explained she was never awake before five. She knew if he came while you were on duty she wouldn't have a chance."

"She can save her ammunition, Davis," Roberta said scornfully. "Any man who would fall for Mrs. Winslow would certainly have no appeal for me. And as for looks, Davis, I'm not much of an admirer of her type. Give me the honest wholesomeness of the girls here in Rebecca Moore. If I happened to be a man I wouldn't hesitate one minute."

The other shook her head. "If you were a man you'd be a fool for a pretty face—plus a fat bank roll—just like the others are. Men aren't interested in brains or wholesomeness when looks are around. I'm not being cynical or sour grapesy, Cameron, I'm just being sensible. That's why our charming divorcée is nice to me and nasty to you, my dear. And if you look at it in that light, she is paying you a compliment."

"I don't want her compliments," Roberta replied, "and she need have no fear I shall ever be a rival. I'm not interested in anything she has or does. I'm her nurse by assignment, not by choice."

She repeated this to herself as she took a few turns up and down the long corridor. Oh, well, she was to sit up for a while this afternoon and maybe would go home at the end of the week. There was little or nothing they could do for her at the hospital—at least nothing but what could be done by her own maid. Roberta hoped her next case would be someone ill in body rather than in ego.

In the afternoon she settled the patient in a chair near a sunny window and remade her bed with fresh linen. Callers began to arrive early and though most of them lingered but a few minutes, there were four young women who seemed determined to make an afternoon of it. They shouted, laughed, smoked and played pranks on each other. When Roberta suggested Mrs. Winslow had been out of bed long enough for the first day, that lady refused to leave her chair.

"It's just as I told Doctor Nichols, girls," she explained, enjoying Roberta's discomfort, "Cameron is altogether too bossy. I suppose I know when I'm tired without her telling me."

Roberta had closed the door to protect the other patients on the floor against disturbance; but even so she expected someone to complain at the noise. Had these girls no sense at all? She was getting angry.

"I'm afraid you will have to leave now," she told the visitors at last. "We can't have our patient getting excited. Please go at once," she murmured to the one Mrs. Winslow called Liz, and who appeared to be the most sensible of the quartette. "This is her first day out of bed, you see."

"Come on, gals," Liz shouted above the clamor, shrugging into her mink coat. "We're gettin' the bum's rush. We've worn out our welcome already. First thing we know we won't even get in to see our pal here. What is this joint, anyway? An asylum or a jail?"

Paula Winslow's eyes blazed with anger. "Don't you dare go! I'm paying for this room and you can stay just as long as I want you to."

"Oh, no, we can't, darling," purred one of the visitors. "All hospitals have rules and even you will find you must obey them. Anyway, I don't believe he's coming this afternoon so we might as well see what we can find at the Club."

"I think you're mean," Paula pouted. "Next time I come here I'll pick my own companion. Leave me your cigs, Tilly. They confiscated mine. You might just sort of mislay your lighter, too. This is the worst place I've struck yet. I'm getting out as soon as possible—tomorrow if I can work it. 'Bye—if you must go. And lay off Doc. Understand? I saw him first and I swear my claim's legitimate."

They trooped out laughing and Roberta thought: "Just as soon as I get her back to bed, I'll air this room. Why will women use such vile-smelling perfume and smoke such terrible cigarettes? Oh, well, it takes all sorts to make up this funny old world."

Just as Roberta feared, Mrs. Winslow had been lying

down but a little while when she complained of feeling ill—nauseated. She began to cry and begged for the doctor.

Roberta called the resident and experienced impish delight at the look of loathing the girl gave her when Doctor Lewis, middle-aged and bald, answered the summons. Did she have an idea it would be Doctor Nichols? Well, she got fooled.

"Too much company," the doctor said gruffly. He had known her all her life. "No more today. None this evening. And take those flowers out of here and open the windows. What sort of a gang did you have in here anyway, Pauline?"

"I'm going home tomorrow morning," Mrs. Winslow stated loudly. "I loathe this place. No wonder I'm sick. I detest being fussed over and I hate being treated as if I had broken all the commandments. I'm going home, I tell you."

"Good!" the doctor said heartily. "Best place for you. If I had my way you'd be out at the farm where no one could get at you and where you'd have a chance to think."

"About my sins, I suppose," she sneered.

"It mightn't be a bad idea at that," the resident said, unperturbed. "Now listen to me, Pauline—yes, that's the name you were baptized and that's the name I'm going to call you always whether you like it or not. You'll land in a sanitarium or worse if you don't

[149]

watch your step. Get wise to yourself, girl. No one can burn the candle twenty-four hours a day without paying for it. Take my advice and go out to the farm—sleep ten or twelve hours a day. Play in the snow. Skate, ski and slide down hill. I bet in a month's time you won't know what a nerve is. How about it? "

" Mother's been talking to you, hasn't she? " the girl asked, glaring at the doctor with over-bright eyes. " She and Dad want to go to Florida. Well, why don't they go? Who's stopping them? "

The doctor got to his feet. " Give her one of these tablets with a little water now and another in an hour if she isn't sleeping." He walked to the door and turned to look back at her. " Behave yourself, baby, and go out to the farm tomorrow. I'll tell your dad you'll go."

Mrs. Winslow refused to answer and Roberta wondered if she actually would go. She very much doubted it. But what a disagreeable girl she was! She had heard the Carlings were perhaps the wealthiest family in the county. Their only son had been killed in an automobile accident and their only daughter was certainly no comfort to them. In Roberta's opinion they were poor indeed.

The next day Paula Winslow left the hospital in the ambulance. Doctor Lewis accompanied her and Roberta wondered if he took her to the farm as he had threatened.

Chapter 13

"DID YOU EVER HEAR OF MARTHA BLACK FISK, BOB?"
Cynthia Cooper asked as she burst into Roberta's room
one mid-afternoon in early February. "And have you
seen the latest addition to our exclusive circle? Rhoda
Deland, *femme fatale*, and I hereby register my extreme dislike of her."

"Her? Who?" Roberta went on buffing her nails,
her thoughts miles away.

"Rhoda Deland, stupid. She's the new nurse—from
N'Yawk and points north and south. She's a fine one
to let loose among the poor innocent yokels up this
way. If Morrison is wise she'll confine her to the
women's surgical—that'll keep her out of mischief for
a spell. But I have an idea she'll draw the new man
in 117—the playwright."

"A playwright? What's his name? What's the matter with him?" Roberta put aside the buffer and
reached for a file.

"Fisk—Martha Black Fisk's husband—she's the painter."

Roberta shook her head. "Never heard of either of them."

"Such ignorance!" Cynthia declared, then: "Neither did I until Austin told me. She's on days. He wrote a lot of wild stuff that has 'em in the aisles, so *she* said. I saw Martha—she's little and sweet. Austin says the man's a big horse. Ever notice how the loveliest women seem to draw that type of man—and like it? But aren't you interested in our blessed event? The advent of the hussy, Bob?"

"Talk English, Cyn," Roberta admonished. "What hussy? What blessed event? Is it quintuplets this time? Rebecca Moore will get a place in the sun if that's the case."

"Quintuplets!" scoffed Cynthia. "Honestly, Bob, one has to parse and analyze a sentence for you before you know what a person's talking about. It's the new nurse—this Deland everyone is discussing. You'll see her at dinner tonight—unless she's off somewhere with one of the doctors. She's that sort—a man's gal, and while it isn't encouraged—that sort of thing—she's the type to get away with it."

"Oh, Cyn, sometimes I can't make head or tail of what you're talking about. I take it the lady is beautiful?"

"Beautiful? I suppose so. If you care for that type.

[152]

She looks like a madonna but I'll bet my last dollar the gal has lived. The way she lifts and lowers her lashes is something to see. I watched her while Jitney talked to her and I had the feeling there was more to that conversation than would sound well before an audience. Jitney doesn't like me any better than I like him and the dirty look he sent in my direction should have shriveled me but served only to strengthen my suspicion they had met before. Do you like him, Bob?"

"Who? Oh, why, yes," Roberta answered carefully. "Of course he is still comparatively new here and has to sort of feel his way."

"Yes," Cynthia snorted derisively, "I noticed that trait in him, and if there is one thing more than another that I detest in a man it's pawing—patting— touching. That's why I like Holmes in spite of his crabbiness—he keeps his hands where they belong."

Roberta hastened to change the subject. "Is this Deland the playwright's special?"

"No doubt she'd like to be, all right. Do you know, Bob, she's too sophisticated for Rebecca Moore. I heard one of the girls say there was talk of replacing Morrison—that a member of the Board favors a younger woman—a disciplinarian. I've been wondering if this Deland might perhaps be the answer. Gosh, I hope not."

"Oh, I doubt if the Board would let Morrison go," Roberta said. "She's really marvelous. You know,

Cyn, we never have any friction here. Are you sure this new girl isn't a special?"

"She's just a lowly member of the staff, even as you and I, Bob," Cynthia assured her, "but oh, so different—so—oh, wait until you see her. I don't know who's on nights. You see, he came only this morning. Maybe they do have a special for nights, but I'm sure it's not Deland."

"What's the matter with him?"

"Observation. Austin said the symptoms all point to a brain disturbance. From what she told me of the stuff he writes I should think he's due for a psychopathic hospital. Why they brought him here when New York was so much nearer, is beyond me."

Roberta sat up, her face eager. "Brain disturbance? Then it's because of Holmes. Probably a growth of some kind. Oh, I hope I get a chance to help. I don't care in what capacity. The last time Holmes did a brain surgery I was suture nurse and it was the biggest thrill of my life. Why, Cyn, it was a miracle performed right before our eyes. Here the man was practically blind and fast losing the use of one arm and leg. After the X-rays, Holmes went to work. He had to probe so deeply to get every bit of the tumor that we all held our breaths lest those quick, deft fingers let the scalpel slip. Of course it didn't slip and Charlie Moulton can thank God and Rebecca Moore's Theron Holmes."

"They are to X-ray this Fisk some time today,"

[154]

Cynthia said. "It seems he's been wretched for some time—losing weight, bad color, loss of appetite, general upset, I guess. I understand his wife thought it might be mastoid because of the soreness behind the ear. But he's sure it's a tumor and refused to have any other advice. Holmes or no one. It seems the pain has been increasing until he gets practically no rest or sleep—so *he* says. She's probably the one who gets none—I'm willing to discount his assertions. If he's as hard-boiled as they say he is, Austin will drive him crazy. She's the limit! So sweet and helpful—dearie this and dearie that. It's nauseating!"

Roberta laughed. "Honestly, Cyn, you're funny. Just because you don't like Austin, you refuse to see her as a splendid nurse. Why, she gets some of the worst cases—she can do just about anything. It doesn't matter where she is placed she somehow manages to come through with flying colors. Someone told me she has never lost a patient. If that's true it must be a record."

"Nuts!" the other scoffed. "Know why she never loses a case, stupid? I'll enlighten you. When things reach a climax, she always manages to have someone with her—a junior nurse, usually. You can call it luck if you like. I call it preparedness. Then she gets a sudden ache somewhere—toothache or something—just about the time the patient gets ready to kick the bucket. I've seen her actually turn green around the gills as the end approached. Maybe she can't help it;

but I'm pretty skeptical because she keeled right over and apparently passed out of the picture once upon a time, leaving me to ease the patient out on his last journey. It didn't spoil her record because I fought for that man's life as I never fought before. He lived two days while Austin nursed acute indigestion, and I heard his daughter say it was a pity Miss Austin was ill because the family had such confidence in her. Of course Lewis knew the man was bound to go and told me not to notice remarks like that; but I tell you, Bob, it rankled. You should have seen the candy and flowers they sent her. Gorgeous! I think Austin's a fake but so far she has managed to fool everyone. If she can get away with it, why more power to her, sez I; but it's a good thing not many of us are like that—good for the patient, I mean."

"Don't be too hard on her, Cyn," Roberta reproved mildly. Cynthia's bark was always worse than her bite.

"Where do you go next, Bob? Pediatrics? Someone said they're short over in Contagion. I'm glad I'm in Maternity. It's grand knowing the mothers are improving by the minute. And I get a big kick out of watching the fathers acting so darned spoony over them when they call. I always feel terribly sentimental myself when I'm over there. It's a good thing Homer's in Chicago or I might break down and say 'yes' some day when he's in a proposing mood; the poor gink isn't in position to marry right now."

"For Pete's sake, Cyn, why not? Homer has a good job——"

"Ma must take the baths at Saratoga and Sister wants to study art. Blah! She ought to be sent to business school and taught the money she'll need to gratify her artistic yearnings, if any, won't be picked off bushes—it'll come out of her long-suffering brother's hide. They make me sick. He does, too, sometimes, for being such a goop."

"Now you're just talking," Roberta said. "Homer doesn't make you sick—ever. He's a prince and don't you dare let him get away from you or you'll regret it all your life. Why don't you marry him? Mrs. Page's ailments are all imaginary—just neurotic nonsense. If she had to get out and hustle you'd see she'd forget all her aches and pains. As for Phyllis, she's pretty and popular and will no doubt marry young. After all, Cyn, you're not taking such great chances."

"Practically none, darling, only I'm not going to point out the idiosyncrasies of a mother and sister and expect to keep the wide-eyed adoration of the son and brother. Ah, no, my child. I know human nature and I know men. Homer and I will just drift along until he wakes up all by himself or until Ma lands a second husband and Phyllis gets a first. I hope, though, I won't lose my hair and teeth before they decide to enter matrimony."

"I've been going to ask about Mrs. Benson. How is

she? Did she go to Florida as Lewis suggested or back home?" Roberta asked. "How she ever managed to finish those two luncheon sets in the short time she did amazes me. I'm taking mine to Beth when next I have time off. She will adore it."

"Mrs. Benson's in Florida until the first of May. She sends me the quaintest little notes—all about how to keep a husband happy. I think you worry her, Bob—with your icy virginity, or, as we moderns say, sex blindness. After all, my dear, you are a woman and a very lovely one and so my advice to you is: better keep that luncheon set yourself," Cynthia said. "Just what's wrong with you, anyway? And why are you so disinterested in the genus homo as a possible meal ticket? Don't tell me you are misguided enough to want to spend your life nursing in a hospital, or even doing private work."

"Oh, probably I was dropped on my head when I was a baby," Roberta shrugged. "Somehow men as such don't interest me. As patients I find them interesting if unreasonable and exasperating." She laughed a trifle ruefully. "I suppose you can't understand that, can you?"

Cynthia shook her head. "I can't. It's unnatural. I guess it's just as Mrs. Benson said. The right man hasn't yet come within your range of vision. According to her, one look is enough. Did you ever see her husband—the late Major? She showed me his picture.

[158]

He certainly was no prize beauty but there was mischief in his eye and a funny quirk to his big mouth. I can quite understand her calling him a crooked stick and also her complete devotion to him. Sometimes I wish Homer wasn't so good-looking."

" Why, for heaven's sake? "

" Well, the women all give him the eye, and while he appears to be quite unconscious of their come hither glances, there may come a time when he'll wake up and then where shall I be? I'm perfectly aware I'm not at all pretty, Bob, and sometimes I wonder just what he sees in me."

Roberta laughed affectionately and patted her friend's cheek. " He sees just what the rest of us do, darling. You're clever and funny and wholesome and *I* think you're beautiful."

" Thanks, Bob, only I think you're a sweet liar. But I'm glad love suffers from astigmatism and I hope Homer never puts specs on or I'm sunk."

At dinner that evening, Roberta met the new nurse and was struck by her unusual beauty. Miss Deland was tall and what was once called willowy. Her eyes were long and dark, heavy lidded and never really open. She had regular, almost classic features and smooth black hair which she wore combed straight back from her face and coiled low in her neck. Not a girl in a thousand would dare wear such a coiffure, but it somehow became Rhoda Deland. She was quiet, almost aloof, and Roberta noticed the interest she aroused in the others. Sitting with slightly bowed head, her profile had a puritanical look and Roberta wondered at the veiled hostility some of the girls displayed.

"Welcome to Rebecca Moore, Miss Deland," she said as they left the dining room side by side.

"Thank you," the other answered and without a glance walked away.

Cynthia Cooper giggled. "Friendly soul, isn't she—to us females? Wonder how on earth she happened to pick Rebecca Moore?"

"Probably for the same reason you and I did—Doctor Theron Holmes," Roberta replied. She felt rebuffed. Yet, perhaps the girl felt the curiosity of the others and resented it.

"Not that one," Cynthia insisted. "There's more to this than meets the eye, my friend. She trained in one of the big New York hospitals and Garsden's a long way from New York. I wonder if rumor is correct this time. One thing's certain that gal's been around and I'll bet my shirt it's not always to prayer-meeting, either. Well, I love a mystery and we shall see."

"She doesn't get nights in 117 anyway," Roberta said, "because I'm going on right away. And she is beautiful, Cyn."

"You are? But —— Do you really think she's beautiful, Bob? She reminds me of a panther. But I suppose a panther is beautiful if you care for that sort of beauty. I don't. That madonna expression comes from having the right kind of nose and straight dark hair. Don't let it fool you—and better watch out for her." Cynthia's voice sank to a whisper. "Lady," she murmured to the back of the oblivious and now completely vanished Deland, "I don't like you at all."

"Oh, you and your mysteries!" jeered Roberta as she left the elevator at the second floor. "You'll get your fingers burned and your nose tweaked some fine day when you're playing detective."

"I suppose that's what comes of reading to the youngsters over in Pediatrics," Cynthia replied, going up to the next floor. "I'm going back there after this night trick in Maternity is over. S'long!"

Chapter 14

CYNTHIA CREPT INTO ROBERTA'S ROOM ONE MORNING just as Roberta was settling herself to sleep. It had been a hard night. 117 had been restless and irritable. Besides the abscess in the ear and acute sinusitis, the examination had revealed a kidney disturbance together with general debility. Harper Fisk had been a very sick man for days. Now with returning vitality, he demanded writing material and insisted he must sit in a chair. Roberta arranged his bed so he could use the rack with greater ease while he regaled her with his ideas of hospitals and doctors in general and this specific institution and staff in particular. Stopping every few minutes to mutter imprecations on everything, he managed to cover several sheets of paper, then in voluble disgust tore what he had written into a dozen pieces. Roberta offered to help. He stared at her as if he thought she had suddenly lost her mind.

"I can take notes," she told him. "My shorthand

may not be the most rapid in existence, but at least I can read it. I can even type, too. But the system I use is the regular business Gregg and your secretary or any typist can put my notes in shape for you."

"Fine!" he snorted angrily and Roberta thought: "What's the use?" He threw paper and pencil to the floor and shouted: "Get a notebook, then. What are we waiting for?"

Roberta retrieved the discarded writing material and sat down beside the bed. "Ready, Mr. Fisk." She sat alertly in her chair, pencil poised for action.

He dictated for two hours and Roberta wondered as she listened just what it was that made his plays click. It all sounded like twaddle to her. After a while he stopped abruptly.

"Now let's see if you are as good as you say you are. Read it."

It wasn't easy. Some of the terms were unfamiliar to Roberta but she managed to wade through page after page expecting every minute to be told to take the stuff away—burn it. But he listened until the end and then laughed uproariously.

"By Jiminy, I've got something there!" he chortled. "Now type what you've done—right away. I want to see how it looks."

Roberta shook her head. "I can't do that, Mr. Fisk," she said reasonably. "I'm a trained nurse, not a secretary."

[163]

"Nurse be damned!" he shouted. "You type those notes. Do as I tell you or you're fired."

"Then I'm afraid I'm fired, because I have no intention of typing those notes either now or at any time." Her voice was low but firm.

The man glared at her malevolently for a long moment. Roberta wondered if he contemplated getting out of bed and, perhaps, leaving the room, and it was three o'clock on a chilly March morning. She spoke crisply—authoritatively.

"I think you have done enough for one night."

"Oh, you do, do you? And who do you think you are to tell me when I've done enough?"

"No one of the least importance, Mr. Fisk, except that I happen to be your nurse and am supposed to see you obey doctor's orders and not undo all the good the treatment here has accomplished. Of course it is entirely up to you whether you leave at the end of two weeks or stay on indefinitely. Another thing; getting angry isn't helping your heart any. Your pulse is much too rapid and it wouldn't surprise me at all if you were running a temperature."

Still staring fixedly at her, the man's face changed. An expression of surprise wiped the petulance from it and he grinned.

"That's telling me," he said. "Okay, lady—let's call it quits, shall we? Leave those notes here and I'll give 'em to Marty when she comes in. She'll get 'em typed for me." He yawned widely. "Guess I'm more tired than I thought."

Roberta lowered his bed and pulled the blankets up around his shoulders. His ear had drained satisfactorily, his color was better and everything pointed to a complete recovery. She wondered just what she would have done if it had been the dreaded brain tumor and he had been doomed to absolute quiet for weeks on end. Sometimes she thought he was actually disappointed that his diagnosis had been wrong and ashamed to have made a fuss over what he considered very common ailments.

"Are you just in, Cyn?" Roberta asked, sitting up in bed. "If you intend staying a while, kindly shut that window."

"No, I got in soon after three," Cynthia replied, lowering the window with a soft swish. "I had a swell time, Bob, and guess whom I saw over in Corinth at the Cosmopolitan. The little number you had last winter—you know, the grass widder—Paula—Paula Winslow. And guess who she was with. Now this is news, baby, and you'd better prepare yourself for a shock."

"Well? Who was it?"

"Jitney—Doctor Nichols!"

"Who? What did you say?"

"I said, his nibs—Nichols. I didn't want him to see

me and I don't think he did. Homer's clever and knew how to maneuver it so we kept to the opposite side of the room from them. There was an awful mob there anyway. But can you tie that?"

"Oh, you must be mistaken, Cyn," Roberta protested with a feeling of dismay.

"Not me, little one. And I wouldn't put anything past him after seeing him and Deland having a *very intimate conversation* in the linen room last week," Cynthia went on. "Either she's a fast worker or they're old cronies. I rather favor the latter supposition. Wait until the chief hears about it, Bob. Then watch the fur fly. They say he adores that niece of his."

Roberta was too stunned to speak. Only last week Stan had twitted her with backing down on her promise to help him—to at least be his friend. He had asked her to drive to Wayland with him to see a patient and she had refused. Was this in retaliation? Not at all likely. She acknowledged to herself that it wasn't so much that she didn't trust him as that she didn't trust herself. His charm was still so potent as to weaken her resistance. She had tried to face it as her father had taught her to face all temptations and perplexities; but she felt her safest course lay in complete alienation. She had offered friendship. How naïve! It was not—it could not be true she had the power to prevent him hurting his wife and ruining his career. The idea was absurd. Anyway, it was no doubt just a coincidence that he and Mrs. Winslow were at the Cosmopolitan. They might not have been together—or even in the same party. As for that "very intimate conversation in the linen room" Cynthia spoke of—that was undoubtedly exaggerated.

"Go to bed, Cyn," she advised, sliding down beneath the covers. "You're dreaming, and for heaven's sake don't repeat what you just told me. It will only get you into trouble. No one will believe you. And please open the window again."

Cynthia stood up. "Is that so? Do you believe me? I see you don't and in that case I have nothing more to say. But don't be surprised at anything that happens, Roberta Cameron." The window went up with a bang—the door slammed shut, and Roberta knew Cynthia was peeved at her reaction to the gossip, for gossip she felt sure it was. Roberta was very tired and in spite of the persistent questions nagging her, she fell asleep soon after Cynthia left.

During the remainder of Harper Fisk's stay in the hospital, Roberta had no more trouble with him. He was gruff and demanding, but she could always get him to do what she felt was necessary. Austin, however, was worn to a frazzle. Every evening when she went off duty she declared she was through, but she appeared next morning wearing the look of a martyr about to be tossed to the hungry lions. With her reputation for getting out of unpleasant cases, Roberta wondered why it was she continued to stick to 117 and concluded it was Martha who kept her on the job.

After Harper Fisk's departure, Roberta was on night duty in Pediatrics. She enjoyed being with the children and after the last drink of water and final alcohol rub for the night, there was very little disturbance.

She had been in Pediatrics a day or two when she received a note from Sylvia Nichols inviting her to tea. During the months of the Nichols' residence in Garsden, Roberta had caught but brief glimpses of Stan's wife. The nurses who had seen her said she was pretty in a flower-like way but aside from Miss Morrison who spoke adoringly of her, no one really knew her.

Roberta rather dreaded this encounter. And yet perhaps if she came to know Sylvia, she might understand something of Stan's problem and apparent unrest. On the afternoon in question she dressed carefully and walked the short mile to the Holmes mansion. She hoped Stan would not appear. It would be much easier meeting Sylvia alone.

She was ushered immediately into the drawing room—a lovely, not too formal room, with a glowing fire and flowers everywhere. Stan's wife came forward with outstretched hands. She was a tiny girl with pale gold hair and wide, childish blue eyes and yet Roberta knew she was in her late twenties. Only her mouth showed maturity and that bore signs of pain and suffering endured over a long period of time. She drew Roberta to a seat on the sofa beside her.

"Uncle Doc has talked so much about you, Miss Cameron, that I felt I must know you. My husband, too, said he had met you one summer when he spent a day or two upstate. He was so delighted when he found you were here. I meant to invite you before, but perhaps you know I am not very strong and while the spirit is willing, the flesh is annoyingly weak. I hope you will forgive me."

"There is nothing to forgive, Mrs. Nichols," Roberta said, and thought: "How can he help loving her?" Aloud she went on: "I have been very busy—we all have, at the hospital this winter."

"I know. You girls are wonderful! Uncle Doc thinks he has the finest staff of nurses in the world."

"And we are sure we have the finest chief," Roberta assured her warmly. "In fact, your uncle is the reason why I chose to come to Rebecca Moore Memorial. I admire his work. We are all very proud to be associated with him."

Mrs. Nichols' laughter was like the faint tinkle of silver bells. "Now that we have that off our chests, let's talk about us, shall we? There isn't much to say about me, except that I'm Stan's wife; but you live such an interesting life. Just why did you decide to become a nurse?"

"I don't know exactly," Roberta said, the words

"I'm Stan's wife," said so proudly and happily, blurring her thoughts. "I imagine I always wanted to."

"I wanted to fly; but this silly old heart of mine keeps me earthbound. I have never even been in a plane. Have you?"

"Yes. Several times. I wanted to be an air hostess; but the family vetoed it. Families have a way of stepping in between a girl and her dreams; making an alteration of plans necessary."

"You are lucky to have a family. My father died during my freshman year at college. But I was always glad he knew and approved of Stan. I think that had something to do with my accepting him so promptly, although we had always been playmates and I suppose had loved each other long before we were aware of it. Father always admired ambition and initiative—in others. Perhaps because there was no incentive for either in his own life."

Roberta thought: "This is an old story to me. I heard it first under very different circumstances. Then, I was the girl Stan loved and wanted to marry." But there was no necessity of saying anything aloud for a maid arrived with tea and they talked of other things. Roberta discovered Sylvia was lonely. She wanted someone to talk to. And although she asked innumerable questions, she seldom waited for an answer.

"Tell me about your meeting with Stan, Miss Cameron," she said abruptly, then laughed in sudden embarrassment. "Do you think I'm silly? Perhaps I am where Stan's concerned. I was about seven when I first saw him looking through the fence bars at me. He was such a handsome boy and—and—well—so forlorn and yet terribly proud. From that day I was his slave and he my Galahad." She laughed again, softly, and laid a small hand on Roberta's. "My dear, I feel as if I had known you always. Will you be my friend, Roberta? I have few intimate friends—I can give so little and—friendship means giving as well as receiving."

Roberta pressed the hand she held. "I shall be proud and happy to be your friend, Mrs. ——"

Sylvia's fingers touched her lips before she could continue. "I want you to call me Sylvia—and I hope you will run in often. Stan is so busy—I see so little of him. And yet, I wouldn't have it otherwise although sometimes I am very lonely." The pensive voice faltered and a low rippling laugh came from the lovely mouth. "Don't ever marry a doctor, Roberta," she warned, "unless there is not the slightest trace of jealousy in your make-up."

Roberta laughed with her. "My dear," she said, "I have no intention of marrying anyone—for a long time—least of all a doctor. We nurses get sort of fed up with men—even doctors."

Sylvia's face sobered. She looked every one of her twenty-eight or nine years. "I wish I could have a child, Roberta," she said sadly. "I tried to break the engagement as soon as I knew—but Stan refused to give me up. Perhaps I was selfish to yield to him; but I loved him."

Roberta's thoughts were chaotic. She must say something. "Perhaps—adoption of a child——" she suggested, thinking: "Stan lied to me."

"Neither Uncle Doc nor Stan will consent to that. They insist I'm not strong enough—I couldn't endure the constant excitement and confusion children bring."

Roberta thought: "The girl is terribly alone. Surely Stan must realize that. Why is he off dancing when he might be here with his wife?" and the doubt that had taken root in her consciousness put forth leaves and began to grow.

"But you will grow stronger soon," she said aloud. "It has been lovely meeting you like this, Mrs.—Sylvia. I will run in whenever I can find time and if you need me or want me especially, give your uncle a message or leave a call at the nurses' annex." She stood up. "I must run. Thank you for the delicious tea—I wish I could reciprocate."

She went back to the hospital feeling puzzled. Was it possible for a woman to live with a man and be mistaken as to his feelings for her? Or was Stanley a better actor than she thought? How did he manage to keep his wife from knowing he had no love for her—that his heart belonged to another girl—if it actually did? And how could he help loving Sylvia?

She was so sweet, so gentle and so lovely. Roberta felt depressed. She wished she had left Rebecca Moore when she had wanted to. Perhaps even now it wasn't too late.

That night she sat beside a homesick boy and told stories until at last he slept. There were tears on the lad's flushed cheeks and his breath came in broken sobs. But he was exhausted with crying and would probably sleep for hours. Poor little chap! The cast on his back would become more comfortable as he grew used to it. The first few days were always the hardest in such cases and the nurses dreaded them; but after a bit the patients usually became philosophical and even contented. Two other children in the ward were in casts and sleeping like cherubs.

At two o'clock the ambulance left the courtyard and every car in the big garage followed. She went to the window and looked down. The night was inky without moon or stars. The rectangles of light from Receiving showed the white of nurses' uniforms below the dark that would be their capes. There must have been an accident somewhere. She cast an inquiring glance over the beds of sleeping children and slipped into the hall. Clara Bowen was over by the window staring down at the departing cars. Roberta joined her.

"Must have been an accident," she ventured.

"I'll find out," Clara offered, and slipped away. She was back almost at once with the news of a wreck on the Central just beyond the Flats about four miles

[173]

from Garsden. No one seemed to know just how serious it was so they had sent every available nurse and doctor. "Gee, Cameron," she complained, "why didn't they let me go along? I've never seen a railroad wreck."

"I have no desire to see one," Roberta said. "I heard all about the last one they had somewhere near there and believe me we had our hands full when they brought in the injured and dying. It wasn't any picnic, I assure you." Clara was always looking for a thrill of some sort. She wanted to be a surgical nurse but Doctor Holmes did not favor her. She was too enthralled with watching, to feel his need of cooperation.

Cars and ambulance came into the yard only to speed off again. The elevator whirred and stopped at the operating floor. The sounds were muffled but Roberta could visualize the entire proceedings.

Chapter 15

IT WASN'T UNTIL SHE WENT OFF DUTY AT SEVEN THAT Roberta heard any of the details of the accident that had roused the sleeping populace and sent it chasing out to the Flats to hinder, with well-intentioned interference, the work of rescue. Three people killed and some score or more injured—four seriously. One of the injured was a Mrs. Tildon who was on her way to a hospital in New Jersey where she expected to give birth to her first child. She had been taken directly to Delivery. She was very ill but Doctor Holmes expected to save both her and the child who was premature and now in an incubator. Roberta repeated the name after Cynthia.

Tildon? Of course it couldn't be the Mrs. Tildon she had met two years ago. Tildon wasn't an especially uncommon name and even if she did happen to live in New Jersey it didn't necessarily mean she was the same person. But to be on the safe side, she intended keeping away from Maternity. Where was Mr. Tildon? Had he been with her? Apparently not. Later she heard that Mrs. Tildon's husband was flying east from Denver where he was in business.

But the Tildon baby died and Mrs. Tildon made a rapid recovery. It was on the day Mrs. Tildon was to leave the hospital that Roberta saw Bert. She was hurrying along the second floor corridor to the elevator at seven o'clock that evening. A man turned a corner and collided with her, grasping her elbows to prevent her falling.

"Oh, I'm sorry—why, hello! Miss —— How are you?"

Roberta said: "Fine, thank you," and started on. But he barred the way.

"By Jove, I remember now. Mrs. Baxter!" He stared at the uniform and up at her startled eyes. "You, a nurse? Where's Chris? We heard he's back in the States again."

A thousand excuses crowded Roberta's brain. Should she continue the masquerade or should she attempt to explain or deny the whole thing? Either way was risky if what Chris had said about Bert Tildon was true. Bert was waiting, his eyes avid. She said the first thing that came into her head.

"That was all a mistake, Mr. Tildon. We—we discovered it and—well, I'd rather not talk about it, if you don't mind."

[176]

The man's face seemed to shriek with delight. It told her he was glad "the stuffed shirt" had come a cropper.

"I don't blame you, Mrs. Baxter —" Roberta held up her hand.

"Miss Cameron, if you please. That other is just a memory. It is as if I had never borne any but my own name. Please forget it."

"Sure—let me congratulate you, Mrs.—Miss Cameron. Do you know, I admired you immensely that night and couldn't understand how you ever fell for that—that —"

"Please!" begged Roberta, fuming inside. How dared he attempt to vilify Chris Baxter whose little finger was worth more than this Bert Tildon's whole conceited body.

"Okay. But will Marge be surprised to hear this! Have you seen Marge? She didn't mention it. How long you been here? How about coming over with me right now?"

"I'm sorry, but I'm on duty and must hurry. Goodbye, Mr. Tildon. Remember me to your wife." She managed to get away; but she felt his curious gaze following her until a turn in the corridor hid her from his view.

What a thing to happen! She hoped Bert would forget this encounter or at least not mention it until he and his wife were alone or out of the hospital.

Rebecca Moore was opposed to married nurses on its staff and trying to explain the affair would cause not only conjecture but doubt as well.

Upon thinking back over the adventure, Roberta acknowledged to herself that it bore all the earmarks of an intrigue. Oh, why had Chris let her in for anything of the sort? He might have known it was bound to leak out or require an explanation some day. Even if he had explained it to the Tildons—they, too, being stormbound—there was just the chance they might have believed it all perfectly innocent and true. And that would have been all there was to it. In Roberta's experience, she had found it didn't pay to lie. Some way, somehow, explanations were in order and the more explanations the harder to really explain. The way things were now, that harmless, innocent little adventure had taken on the color of an illicit amour. Perhaps she made things even worse by allowing Bert to believe she had divorced Chris. Well, it was Chris's fault—he had no business putting her in such a position in the first place. No matter what he said to the contrary, it was not at all necessary.

Bert said Chris was back in the United States again. She wondered if Bert and he would meet and just what turn their conversation might take. "Oh, what a tangled web we weave when first we practice to deceive." She shook her head as if to clear her mind of this new worry. Where was Chris now? Well, that was one thing over which she need lose no sleep. He didn't know where she was and it was not at all likely they would meet. Anyway, she very much doubted if he even remembered her.

Next afternoon, Roberta answered a summons to the reception room with some trepidation. What now? Helen Donley, whom she had not seen since graduation nearly two years ago, rushed to meet her.

"I couldn't go without saying good-bye, Bob," she said as they settled themselves on the wide sofa.

"Go?" Roberta asked. "But Grandpa will have to postpone his trip abroad this year, won't he?"

"*He* will but *I* won't," Helen answered. "Bob, you'll never guess what's happened. Arnold's heading a hospital unit for work in France and I've joined. We sail on Friday."

"But——" Roberta began.

"Believe it or not, Bob, Grandpa shelled out handsomely. He didn't know I was quitting him; but he managed to weather even that blow, all of which reflects credit on my nursing. Arnold's working without pay—the rest of us for mere living expenses. I'm thrilled and scared and happier than I've been since I was a kid. At last I'll justify my existence, Bob."

Cynthia came in and the story had to be repeated.

"I wonder how it happens that some are chosen for heroic living and others have to serve as sort of a background for them. There was Myrt—and now you."

She bit her lip to still its trembling. "I guess I'm just a dud."

"Oh, you've chosen a real job, Cyn," Helen said, then with a trace of cynicism: "It's up to you and Bob here to provide the future citizens—boys to go to war and girls to mourn them. It's a rotten system, isn't it? Yet we countenance it."

A horn sounded outside and Helen stood up. She flung an affectionate arm about the others. "There's Hamilton. We're on our way to her home. Remember us in your prayers, girls—we'll sure need them."

They watched her as she ran down the walk and climbed into the green coupé. Her hand lifted in farewell and she was gone.

"Another perfectly good nurse laid on the altar of so-called civilization," Cynthia muttered, her eyes bright with tears. "Sometimes I feel like a slacker, Bob, wanting nothing more of life than to settle down with my man and make a home for him and our children. Why am I deaf to the call to go over there? The very thought of all that perfectly useless carnage nauseates me; I can't stand wholesale murder."

"I'm surprised at Helen," Roberta said. "And to think she's going in Arnold's unit! I wonder ——"

"It's not so strange. She's been living right there in Weston. I'm more surprised at Arnold. He had a pretty good job at the hospital. But there it is—the chosen few for the heroic life." She spoke musingly.

[180]

"Come on, Cyn," Roberta said, catching the other's hand. "Let's get out of here for a while. Let's go for a walk."

"Say, Bob, how many secret relatives has the chief got up his sleeve for Pete's sake?" Cynthia Cooper inquired as she strolled into Roberta's room one mid-afternoon.

"I don't know. Has another relative appeared? And just who is it this time and what does it matter, anyway?" Roberta asked.

"Well, he's here in the hospital."

"Oh, it's a he and he's ill, I gather." Roberta was quite unimpressed. "What's he in for?"

"Nephew. I didn't hear his name. He's got an infection—contracted in the jungles of Africa or some place. Bet you a dollar, Deland gets the job nights. She's ace high with Jitney. Austin's on days. What a drag that gal's got!"

Roberta laughed. "There you go again! She must be good or the chief wouldn't give her the job of nursing his nephew. Don't be a crab, Cyn. Some men like the maternal type."

Cynthia hooted derisively. "Fisk didn't. What a life he led her! I wish I could have heard him bawl her out."

Roberta shook her head. "It wasn't at all pleasant, Cyn," she said, "and I should know; for I had a pretty

[181]

large dose of it. The man is quite impossible. Just a big bully who has never yet met his match."

"Did he bawl you out, Bob?" Cynthia asked incredulously. "I don't see how he dared. What did you do? What did he say? I do wish I'd been there! What fun!"

Roberta shrugged slim shoulders. "Oh, the climax came when he demanded paper and pencils and found he couldn't handle them. I had cautioned him against taxing his slowly returning strength, but to no avail. When I suggested that I take down his ideas in shorthand, he decided that as a trained nurse I was a fine secretary and ordered me to type what he had dictated immediately. I refused and he promptly fired me. Of course I didn't stay fired and he came down off his high horse. After that we got along all right in a manner of speaking. How his wife ever stands him beats me."

"Did you see her? Well, wouldn't you know she'd fall for a big gorilla like that? She eats it up—simply adores him and when he roars she rolls her eyes and probably thanks a kind Providence that gave her a Tarzan for a mate. I met her one evening in the hall and honestly all she could talk about was Harper—my husband, Harper Fisk. Sickening!"

"I hope they don't change me again right away," Roberta said. "I love Pediatrics. Timmy Brooks and I are writing a story all about a boy and his dog. Sometimes the other youngsters add their bit; but the tale is really Tim's."

"How about coming downtown with me, Bob?" Cynthia suggested. "There's a suit in Dawsons' I sort of like and I want your opinion. Homer's coming home week after next and I'm invited over for the week end."

Roberta joined her in the lower hall of the hospital and they left by the front entrance opening into broad Main Street. In front of the hospital they came face to face with Doctor Holmes. He greeted them with his usual gruff courtesy and Cynthia wrinkled her nose when they were safely past. They noticed the Holmes limousine drive up to the hospital entrance and stop.

"Oh, I remember now," Cynthia said. "It's this evening Doc goes to Chicago for that ten days convention. He's to read a couple of papers——"

"Doctor Holmes going away?" Roberta was never able to understand how Cynthia managed to gather the information she always had at her tongue's end.

"Oh, yes. He's going. Doc's getting to be quite a big bug these days. Of course it's a grand compliment for Rebecca Moore; but all the same I can't help wishing he wasn't going—just now."

"Why?"

"There's an undercurrent here—something sinister below the bland surface. Can't you feel it?"

Roberta laughed merrily. "Honestly, Cyn, you get

[183]

the darnedest ideas. Certainly I don't feel anything. And what would happen here—that's sinister, I mean?"

"You'll see," was the cryptic answer.

A block from the hospital Doctor Nichols passed in his long gray car without recognition. Cynthia made another face. Roberta laughed but she was slightly piqued. She felt sure Stan's failure to greet them was intentional.

"Is there anyone in the whole hospital you do like, Cyn?" she asked.

"Sure," Cynthia replied promptly. "I like Morrison, I like Lewis and I like you. There are one or two others, but you three are quite enough. The rest can go hang."

The little suit at Dawsons' was pretty and becoming and Cynthia bought it and a perky, crazily impossible hat to go with it. They walked back to the hospital in the early April sunshine—two amazingly attractive girls, each trying to forget the shadow of war that had touched them.

Roberta was changing into her uniform when Clara Bowen stopped in her room.

"Darn it, Cameron," she wailed, "why did they have to change you right now? Cooper and I never get along together."

"Change me? I didn't know." Roberta was sorry. She had hoped to stay on in Pediatrics for some time.

"Don't you ever look at the Bulletin Board?" the other asked.

"Usually," Roberta replied, "but I sort of took it for granted I wouldn't be changed right away. I don't know why. Wishful thinking, perhaps."

"You're on nights in 217—the chief's nephew. It's nothing but an infection. I don't see why he has to have two nurses anyway. Austin says he's not so very sick. Why make a fuss over him just because he's the chief's nephew?" Clara was disgruntled. She and Cynthia Cooper rubbed each other the wrong way.

"Another man!" Roberta groaned to herself. "Probably another spoiled darling." But she knew there was no help for it.

"So you're teacher's pet," Cynthia said as they left the dining room some time later. "I see you draw Uncle's nephew. I wonder what he's like."

Roberta shook her head. "I don't know and I don't care. But I can tell you one thing, I'll stand for no monkey business from him just because he happens to be the chief's nephew. I'm his nurse and he'll do what I say or I'll know the reason why."

"Atta girl!" Cynthia applauded and slapped her smartly on the shoulder. She ran for the elevator. "I'll tell Timmy you're two-timing him," she called, and Roberta shook her head vigorously, getting an impish laugh in return.

"He doesn't need a night nurse any more than a cat

needs two tails," Austin muttered as Roberta entered 217 a few minutes later. "He's quiet—scarcely speaks and has insisted on sleeping practically all day. I tried my best to interest him in something. No sale. He said he was tired and bored. He doesn't like hospitals and is sure the chief ordered him hospitalized so he can keep him from running away. So far he's been quite docile, however, almost too much so, if anything—sort of apathetic."

Roberta smiled. "Well, one would scarcely expect him to be very energetic or buoyant with an infected foot, Austin," she chided.

"Maybe not," the other replied acidly, "but he could at least act as if he was aware I was in the room, couldn't he? If I met him in Egypt, I'd know he was Holmes' nephew—a relative anyway. I think he hates himself."

"Probably he does hate being laid up," Roberta agreed. "He may actually be all vim, vigor and vitality, radiating charm and good will, when he's well."

"I doubt it—the crab!" Austin snorted, as she prepared to leave.

"Sa-ay, Austin," Roberta grinned at the sulky face, "what's become of all that happiness and good cheer you are usually so lavish with? Don't tell me you've mislaid it."

"It's wasted on some of the creatures we get here," she retorted. "Well, here's hoping you enjoy yourself."

[186]

Roberta looked toward the bed. The occupant was tall and, judging by the lean brown hand outside the cover, very thin. He lay on his side, face to the wall, and Roberta supposed he slept. Poor fellow!

Chapter 16

ROBERTA BUSIED HERSELF ABOUT THE ROOM AND WAS startled when a voice said softly:

"So it really is you? I couldn't quite believe it. Hello, Robin! I told you we should meet again."

"Chris!" Roberta whispered and held out her hand. "Then you're—you're——" she stammered, too astonished to talk coherently.

"Christopher Baxter in the flesh," he explained. "Doctor Theron Holmes' only nephew, hence my being put to bed under the stern eyes of two nurses. I told Uncle Doc it was a lot of foolishness; but he insists I'm way below par—probably harboring some bugs of dubious ancestry and in need of a complete going over. Proper rest, diet, etc. Nuts!"

"No doubt he's right," Roberta said.

"I was going over to Bramton in search of your sister. I remember you said her name was Macklin," Chris explained. "Do you know, Robin, I've thought a lot about you. Everywhere I went your face was before me and I wrote you endless letters but never quite had the temerity to mail them. Anyway, I didn't know your address. I hope you thought of me occasionally," he ventured.

"Of course I did," Roberta said, her mind busy familiarizing herself with his case history.

"Oh, ye-ah?" he growled skeptically. "Well, I saw Bert Tildon when I was in Baltimore and, fortunately, was able to dodge him. He's one person I always dodge—if I can."

"You were luckier than I. I ran into him—right here in the hospital," Roberta said ruefully.

"The heck you did!" Consternation showed in his face. "Did he recognize you? What did he say?"

"Of course he recognized me. You don't suppose I've changed much in two years, do you? He was surprised to see me in uniform. He told me you were back in the States. I wondered if you had seen him and what your story was."

"What was he doing in this particular hospital?"

"His wife was in a train wreck over near the Flats and was brought here. He flew east from Denver. I didn't see Mrs. Tildon. I assure you Bert was quite sufficient."

"What did he say to you?"

"He shouted: 'Mrs. Baxter! You—a nurse! Where's Chris?'"

"Yes—yes. Go on. What did you say?" Chris asked anxiously.

"I said: 'That was all a mistake, Mr. Tildon. We discovered it and—I'd rather not talk about it.' Of course he probably thought right away there was a separation or a divorce—I let him think so. I was afraid he would shout it to the populace. I got away as quickly as I could and he went on to tell Marge. They left the hospital that night; but I don't know whom they told. You see, Rebecca Moore doesn't employ married nurses. We are supposed to be wedded to our profession. I'm afraid he hasn't a very high opinion of you. I told you it was all quite unnecessary—inventing that fantastic story. I never expected to meet either of you again and now look what's happened!"

"Oh, your job's safe as far as that goes," Chris told her. "What I can't understand is why it was necessary to let him think we are divorced or separated. It was none of his business. Why didn't you tell him so?"

"Why didn't you two years ago? I mean, let him think what he liked? The whole thing was utterly crazy and I only hope complications won't get worse and worse. I sincerely trust I have seen the last of the Tildons," Roberta said emphatically. She poured a fresh glass of water for her patient.

"There is one way we could shut their mouths, Robin," Chris said tentatively, after a long moment. "We could make it real. You could marry me."

[190]

Roberta stared at him in astonishment. "Marry you?" she gasped. "Why should I marry you?"

"I can think of several reasons why you might consider it. In words of one syllable there's that much used and constantly abused term: 'love,' for instance. I don't suppose you could possibly care two buttons for me— yet; but I improve on acquaintance, Robin. There are people who are really quite fond of me."

"I'm sure there are," Roberta soothed.

"Nothing sure about it," he contradicted promptly. "What is this, anyway? Are you and Uncle Doc in cahoots to humor me—make life easy so I'll be content to stay in this bed forever? Nothing doing. My foot'll be okay in a week. It's only——"

"Don't be a baby!" Roberta said crisply. "I have no intention of humoring you. You're old enough to know that an infection is nothing to fool with. If it gets into the blood stream there'll be trouble. We've got to see that it doesn't."

He lay for a moment watching her as she moved about the room. "Believe it or not," he said at last, "you have never been out of my mind one minute since you left me that night. At first I thought it was just because you were beautiful and a grand sport and then I began to realize it was something more than admiration. I don't suppose you've given me one serious—er—affectionate thought in all that time, have you?" he persisted.

"Why, yes," Roberta said truthfully. " I have thought of you. Quite often, too; but not at all in a sentimental way."

"Well? Will you think of me—that way—now? " he asked.

Roberta shook her head. " I'm sorry, Chris," she replied. " I'm not at all interested in love. I don't want to think about you or any man that way. And now let us forget all this nonsense and get down to business. You know, I have a notion it's your being here— in the hospital, makes you feel sentimental. Lots of men fancy themselves in love with their nurses. Maybe it's the uniform. Fortunately, a nurse seldom falls in love with her patient—in real life. Fortunate for the patient, I mean." She saw a puzzled look dawn in his eyes. " So you're the chief's nephew and you got this infection in South America. Why didn't you take care of it at once? "

"Lord knows how it got hold of me unless as Uncle insists I was below par. I've had blisters before and rusty nails and various bites without losing a minute's work or an ounce of energy but this time it won't heal. I can't shake the darned thing off. So, Uncle Doc ordered me to bed and here I suppose I'll stay until he pronounces my foot cured and my blood count normal. The whole thing makes me irritable and cross. I'll probably be an old bear."

"You're terribly thin," Roberta murmured, then

encouragingly: "But we'll soon have you quite fit again. I'm sure you are going to help."

"Listen, Robin," the man said irritably. "Don't be so darned cheerful. I feel rotten in case you don't know it and everyone has harped on that same old string: 'You'll soon be fit as a fiddle.' I even heard one imbecile say: 'Hospitalization? Oh, hospitalization's just the thing for you—a nice long rest with people catering to your every whim and first thing you know you'll feel like a new man. Lucky stiff to have a hospital-conscious uncle.' Ye-ah? But it isn't a nurse I need so much as someone to let off steam to. I don't think much of Uncle Doc's day choice. Too sugary—too cursed maternal!"

"She's a fine nurse," Roberta said.

"She may be, but I tell you, I don't need a nurse. Uncle Doc insisted on not one nurse but two. It did no good to rebel—anyway, I had reached the point where I didn't care a hoot. When he mentioned you, I said I had met a girl by the same name. He acted peeved. Said from all accounts everyone had met you at some time or other. I don't know what he was driving at. He tried to get out of his bargain to send you here nights, but I insisted it must be you or no one. I didn't know you were a nurse, Robin. You didn't tell me." His voice was aggrieved. "Do you mind taking care of me? I'll try not to be a nuisance."

"Why no, I don't mind," Roberta replied. "Why

[193]

should I? That is why I'm here. Now if you will just take this under your tongue ——"

He made a wry face at her but submitted to the thermometer, rolling his eyes as if the ordeal were painful.

"It's fine the doctor has both you and his niece with him," she said conversationally. "He has been very lonely."

When she removed the thermometer and recorded its reading, he explained.

"Sylvia is Aunt Kathie's niece and I'm Uncle Theron's nephew. We're really no relation but I have always been fond of her. She's a sweet girl and her life is one continuous tragedy—because of the criminal selfishness of —— Oh, let it ride. What's done is done."

Roberta thought: "She is Stan's wife and she loves him. Her life isn't all tragedy." But she said nothing.

"Do you know Sylvia, Robin?"

"I had tea with her a while ago. She is very charming."

"Of course you know her husband, Doctor Nichols? He's on the staff here."

Roberta hoped her face betrayed nothing as she acknowledged she knew Doctor Nichols.

"Merely as consultant," she qualified and trusted that disposed of the subject. She thought of the wedding ring she had been unable to return and said:

"I stopped at the cottage on my way back to the

hospital after the storm. I wanted to return your ring, but you had already gone. I hadn't the faintest idea where to send it so I still have it over in my room. I'll bring it to you tomorrow. It was stupid of me not to have thought of it before I left; but it was all so hurried——"

"Hurried is right. That was the best meal I ever tasted, Robin, although I didn't enjoy it as much as I would have if you had stayed. What was the idea of rushing away like that, anyway?"

"I told you. I was due at my sister's and if I hadn't gone when I did, there was no knowing when I could have reached Shandleys Beach. Tell me, was that place really yours—I mean, did you have a right to be there? I always had a sneaking suspicion you were as much a trespasser as I was. Did you break in?"

"Why, no." He showed surprise at her doubt of him. "I told you it was loaned me by Meta Palmer, who is a remote relative, and that my plans for using it went haywire. Some time I'll tell you about it—the story of my life. I left early next morning."

"And Rufus?"

"I shipped him out to my sister. Orellana wouldn't have agreed with him. Hello, Stan!" Roberta turned as Doctor Nichols came into the room.

"So this is where you are?" the doctor said. "Nice room—and I might add, you have two of our best nurses—Austin and Cameron. You certainly seem to be the fair-haired boy around here. How you feeling, old man?" Not by word or look did he appear to notice Roberta's presence and she told herself firmly it was as it should be.

"So-so," Chris answered laconically.

"Your uncle tells me you and Cameron here are old friends." He cast a fleeting glance at Roberta then concentrated once more on the patient.

"Sure," Chris said. "It's swell seeing her again. How's Sylvia tonight? Head better?"

"H'mm," the doctor murmured examining the chart. "Better not do too much talking, Chris. Quiet and complete relaxation are indicated. I'll leave something to insure him a good night's sleep, nurse. See that he takes it. I know this young fellow." He laid a hand on Chris's shoulder and Roberta was surprised to see Chris draw back from his touch. The thought flashed through her mind that perhaps it was Sylvia for whom Chris entertained romantic notions. But according to Sylvia herself she had always been in love with her husband. In that case, Chris would scarcely have bought a wedding ring and come north in the expectation of marrying her.

Doctor Nichols turned back the blanket and examined the leg above the bandaged foot.

"Uncle Doc saw it just before he left," Chris informed him.

"I know. But these things need watching."

Doctor Nichols departed.

"No dope, Robin," Chris announced flatly. "I probably won't sleep much tonight because I dozed more or less all day. It was defensive. That voice! But what if I don't sleep? It's no killing matter, is it? It makes my head ache to read all the time and I can't stand Araminta. If I turn day into night and vice versa whose business is it?"

"Araminta? You mean Austin? Her name is Edna and really she's a wonderful nurse. There's an interesting legend about her to the effect that she has never lost a patient. Better hold on to her," Roberta warned. She smoothed the bedclothes with capable touches.

"I don't intend ruining her record or spoiling the legend by dying, Robin—not just when I've found you again; but why don't they give her a more serious job than this?"

"I don't know, unless Doctor Holmes wants the very best for you." She laughed into his eyes. "Hence my advent."

"That's okay; but couldn't you be on all the time?"

"Have a heart, man!" the girl exclaimed. "We nurses are human. We have to have some rest, you know. Then, too, you're really not ill enough for constant attention—just spoiled, perhaps. I tell you, suppose I read to you. Tell me what you like in the way of entertainment and I'll send down to the library for it."

"Later. Let's talk for a while, Robin. Tell me everything that has happened to you since—since our all too brief marriage."

"Doctor Nichols says you are to be quiet—relaxed. No, I'd better read and you try to obey orders."

"Phooey to Nichols!" Chris said crossly. "He's not my doctor. Go on—talk, Robin. Did you know that a few years back, that marriage of ours would have been legal—what they used to call a common-law marriage? They were binding, too. But I'm afraid this time it wouldn't hold."

"I should hope not," Roberta exclaimed indignantly. "That was just about the craziest thing I ever heard of. Oh, I hope the Tildons are definitely out of the picture. Did you know that wreck was probably responsible for the death of their baby?"

"Why, no. I hadn't heard there was a baby."

"It lived only a day or two. Premature. Mrs. Tildon recovered very quickly though."

Chris was silent for a moment. "I can't imagine that pair with a child, Robin. Somehow the picture doesn't fit. Marge was probably on her way to New Jersey. Her people live there. She wrote Hilda after they barged in on us, telling her she had met me and my bride. Sis wired me for particulars. I made a clean breast of it to her and she told me I was a fool for not making the marriage legal. She never cared for Gail and she liked my description of you."

"That was sweet of your sister and of you, too; but

a marriage isn't quite so easily arranged. Anyway, I'm not the marrying type. And I still think it was all entirely unnecessary and quixotic. I must remember to return your ring—you may need it some day, though I strongly advise against offering it to every girl with whom you come in contact."

"Suppose you keep it until I call for it, Robin," he said. "It will be safe with you and will sort of serve as a link—make you think of me occasionally. And don't imagine for a moment I would have given it to just any girl who happened to be stranded with me. I'm not that chivalrous. There was nothing quixotic about my giving it to you—just plain necessity."

"Did it belong to your mother, Chris?" Roberta asked. "It's so plain for these days."

"No. It was bought for the girl I expected to marry. I came north for the wedding—as I supposed—only to find the girl had decided she preferred another man. It was news to me. I knew nothing of any changed plans until I arrived in Rochester where only Rufus, whom I had never seen—having bought him from the Russell Kennels by wire for her birthday—gave me a very exuberant welcome. Her mother said Gail wanted me to have him—for remembrance. As for the ring—I hate flossiness in anyone or anything. I always remembered my mother's wedding ring and I got one as near like it as I could. Gail married a local boy—one who will keep her right in Rochester and not expect her to follow him—God knows where, as her mother informed me. Oh, she was kind about breaking the news—she's a kind woman—I understand. Well, there's the complete story of my love-life, up to the time I met Roberta Cameron. I don't stack up very high in the telling, do I? "

"I'm sorry, Chris," Roberta murmured, her eyes sympathetic.

"Don't be," he said brusquely. "It was the best thing ever happened to me. I can see that now, but I confess I was pretty much bowled over just at first. It was queer. I was absolutely sunk when I reached Meta's cottage that afternoon, but after you arrived the depression lifted never to return. You were such a darned good sport, Robin. Do you know, you've never really left me since—in spite of your hasty departure. Somehow, I always sort of resented that extreme haste. It was almost as if you were afraid to stay. Was I at all ogre-ish? "

"Don't be silly," Roberta retorted. "I told you why I left. How did I know the storm was definitely over? I had to get out while the going was good. Then, too, Jeremiah might not have been willing to travel—he gets spells sometimes. In that case, I should have tried to inveigle you into driving me."

"Darn Jeremiah!" Chris growled. "I should adore being inveigled by you." He lay stretched at ease, hands behind his head, eyes reminiscent. "Tell me what you have been doing since you ran out on me. Were you a nurse then or in training?"

"In training," Roberta answered, feeling it useless to insist upon silence. "I finished in June of that year and late in July came here to work under Doctor Holmes. I spent that summer vacation at Shandleys Beach, some four or five miles up the lake from Bramton. Last year I went to Maine. Have you been in South America all the time?"

"Until two weeks ago when I completed that particular job and came home with a bum foot. I'd been feeling rotten for weeks, but made up my mind to stick until the job was finished. The firm's giving me a leave of absence until I'm back on top again. Pretty decent chaps—my bosses."

Chapter 17

IT WAS AFTER MIDNIGHT WHEN CHRIS BAXTER FELL INTO a fitful sleep. Roberta examined the lean brown face against the pillow. There were strength and kindliness in that firm jaw and wide mouth. The broad high forehead and well-spaced blue eyes showed wisdom and humor. His hair was thick and inclined to be unruly and just now a dark shadow lay on cheek and upper lip. She wondered if he would insist on shaving himself. She knew enough about her patient to be sure he would not be a passive one—would not submit to coddling. He had promised to be good. How good? she wondered.

What sort of girl was this Gail who had treated him so summarily? And what kind of man could have made her forget her promise to Chris? Probably one who could provide all the luxuries and security of civilization. No doubt she was scared at the thought of a little discomfort even for the man she had professed to love. Roberta's lip curled in disdain. Coward! Chris was well rid of her. Some day he would find a girl who appreciated him; who would be willing to devote her life to making him happy and contented. He said the meal she had prepared so many months ago was the best he had ever eaten. It had been fun getting it ready. Of course he had not been serious when he asked her to marry him. Why, he didn't know her. No doubt it was due to the lonely life he had been living and his illness. She should dislike hurting him— he was such a dear! Unconsciously, she sighed.

Doctor Nichols stopped in for a moment on his way back from the operating room. He had performed an appendectomy on the city's mayor, the outcome of which was uncertain because of his general condition. *He* had performed it. But was Stan a surgeon? Evidently.

"It's criminal to allow oneself to go like that," he muttered. "The fool tried to excuse himself on the score Doc had always pulled him through; but it didn't go down with me. He wanted Doc—his old pal, but I ordered him to the hospital instantly and here's hoping he pulls out of it."

"But if Doctor Holmes didn't think he could stand an operation or ——" began Roberta, forgetting her place in her anxiety lest something go wrong during the chief's absence.

"I don't understand why Holmes hasn't operated

[203]

before," the doctor interrupted, frowning. "He's had these recurring attacks for years, his wife told me. The only excuse I can see is Doc's not as young as he once was and may be getting away from surgery. Maybe it's a good thing I came when I did, though I'm frank to say I hesitated. However, it will no doubt work out all right." He shrugged and motioned toward the bed where Chris lay, breathing quietly. "No sense in your being on this job," he said. "Chris doesn't need a night nurse, and anyway, one of the other girls would have answered the purpose. Just why did Doc insist on your being on this particular job—nights?"

Roberta shook her head, a warning finger on her lip. "After all, he is Doctor Holmes' nephew and I suppose he feels anxious about him."

"Doc's an old fuss-budget where his family is concerned. I told him Chris would be all right now he is away from that foul job. It will take time, to be sure; but there's no sense in coddling the chap. But no, Doc insists on day and night attendance. What do you think of Chris, Berta?"

"Oh, I don't know," she murmured, purposely misunderstanding his question. "He is very thin and it looks to me as if hospitalization is the very best thing that could happen to him. So far he has been a model patient, but of course it is early to say, definitely."

"Look, Berta," he whispered, "come outside for a moment. I want to talk to you."

Reluctantly and ashamed of the sudden lift to her heart, she followed him into the corridor. Carson, the floor nurse, was sitting within range of vision and Stanley took a stand with his back toward her. In spite of the feeling of excitement his presence always gave her, she couldn't help experiencing relief that Carson was there. It was so easy to start gossip in a small place like this and she wanted none of it.

"Well?" she asked as Stanley hesitated and cast a belligerent eye over his shoulder.

"If I meet you down by the Library this afternoon about four, will you come for a ride? I must talk to you, Berta. There are going to be changes here—it is as much to your advantage as to my own and the future of Rebecca Moore. Will you do it? I can get you back in time to go on duty and no one need ever know. Anyway, why wouldn't it be all right? You've got a swell standing in the hospital. Why not trust me, Berta? Some day you'll be glad you did. There's a quiet Inn out West Lake Turnpike where we might even dance."

What was he hinting? What was going on here? He was waiting for her answer; but of course she had no intention of going with him.

"Please don't ask me to do such things, St—Doctor Nichols, for you know I can't," she said steadily, her voice low.

"Okay," he muttered sullenly. "I never supposed

you were a prude, Berta. What harm is there in your riding with me occasionally, or even in having dinner? This is 1940, girl. People don't pay any attention to such things nowadays. I thought you liked me—once you confessed you loved me. Has it vanished completely, Berta?"

Roberta took a step toward the door. "I asked you not to speak of that again, Doctor," she rebuked him. "You gave me your word not to refer to it ——"

"I told you I needed you and you stayed. Are you going to renege now—the first time I have asked you to help me? Why did you stay if ——"

"I stayed because both you and Doctor Holmes persuaded me I was needed here," she said with something of her old spirit. Then, impulsively, she said with a little rush of words: "I have met your wife. I—she is sweet, Stan. How can you ——"

He drew back. "You're small-town, Berta. I never thought of you as provincial before, and please don't try to drag Sylvia into this. I know my wife—this has nothing to do with her ——"

"But it has everything to do with her. You can't hurt her—she adores you ——"

Carson looked up from the table. Roberta felt her curious gaze upon them—she knew she was straining her ears. She must end this senseless conversation at once. Carson was an old gossip.

"I'm sorry, Stan," she murmured, then distinctly:

"I'll see he follows the schedule prescribed, Doctor," and slipped through the door.

Her heart was beating irregularly. He thought she didn't want to go with him but poor fool that she was, she did! Was it just because she was small-town that she refused to submit to his attentions, or was it because she felt it was wrong to play with fire? Wrong and dangerous. And since she had met Stan's wife she felt more keenly than ever the necessity of holding herself aloof from his too ardent friendliness. She knew she could never do anything to hurt Sylvia Nichols.

She closed the door softly behind her, only to hear her patient ask petulantly, "Has he gone? What were you two whispering about out there? I'm not going to take any dope, Robin, so you may as well make up your mind to it first as last." Roberta wondered how much Chris had heard.

"Dope? We don't give dope here, Chris. This is just a mild sedative and if you are wise you will take it."

"Nothing doing. Anyway, I wouldn't let Stan doctor me—or a sick cat—unless I wanted to get rid of it." His tone was bitter.

"Oh, come now," she said as to an irritable small boy. "That's not fair. Doctor Nichols is a fine doctor. Already he is popular, not only here but in the entire county."

"With a lot of empty-headed females, maybe. He

should have stayed with Massy and his neurotic women. He's too good-looking for a general practitioner. He ought to go to Hollywood. I suppose you, too, think he's handsome, don't you, Robin?" he asked, turning restlessly to the other side of the bed.

"Well, yes, I suppose he is," Roberta answered as if she hadn't given the subject much thought. "But a person's looks don't matter so much, do they?"

"I hope not," he told her fervently. "Try to keep Nichols away from me as much as you can, will you? We never got on. But no doubt you're quite aware of it by this time. Believe it or not, Robin, I even tried to prevent his marrying Sylvia. He's just not the right sort."

Roberta recalled Stan's story of his wretched childhood; of being brought up by neighbors, poor as himself, and of the generosity of the girl who later became his wife. Stan couldn't help being born on the wrong side of town—of the wrong kind of parents. Her eyes blazed with sudden scorn. "That's a perfectly rotten thing to say, Chris Baxter," she said sharply. "I didn't think you could be such a snob."

"H'mm," Chris mused, looking puzzled. "Just how do you mean—snob? And what do you know about Stanley Nichols, anyway?"

"Please don't let us discuss Doctor Nichols, Chris," she said hastily. "After all, you know, I'm a member of the staff and it isn't ethical to repeat or listen to

[208]

disparaging remarks about any member of it. You do understand, don't you?"

"Oh, sure," Chris said shortly. "My error, Robin. Far be it from me to debunk the hero of a thousand heartbeats. Put that lousy book away. I don't want to be read to. And don't think you have to be pleasant to me. I hate forced pleasantry and I hate people who move about stealthily. I'm not dying and I don't want to be treated as if I was something fragile." He turned on his side, smothering an oath as pain shot through his foot, and pulled the bedclothes close about his shoulders.

"Go on," he prompted. "Tell me what a grand guy Nichols is. Rave along to your heart's content and see if I care. You're just like all the rest—fall for a fine profile and a smooth line."

And Roberta, the model nurse, lost her temper. "So that's the way you cooperate! Is this being as good as possible? If it is, I can't say I blame Gail whoever-she-is for preferring another man."

She laid the offending volume on the table and sat down with a late copy of *The Journal of Nursing*.

"All right. She's lucky. So what?" came in muffled tones.

Roberta disdained to carry the conversation further and silence reigned until Chris's deep, regular breathing proclaimed him asleep.

Roberta bit her lip to hide a smile. When ill or uncomfortable, even the best of men were apt to be little better than spoiled brats. She knew Chris felt wretched. Tomorrow he would be ashamed of his childishness—that is, if he was feeling better, and it was quite in the nature of things that he might.

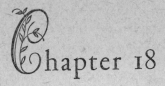

Chapter 18

SEVEN O'CLOCK FOUND THE MOOD OF THE PATIENT IN 217 still peevish. He submitted to the usual morning ministrations of his night nurse with poor grace.

"I suppose you're glad to get away," he growled, as Roberta made a final notation on his chart. "Sorry I'm so repulsive to you."

"I'll excuse that because I can appreciate the present state of your temper is due to your physical condition and because I know you are normally a very pleasant person," Roberta said calmly.

"Umph! I notice you're always in a great rush to put as much distance as possible between you and this 'very pleasant person.' Of course I realize I'm just an ordinary engineer—a rough chap without one single claim to charm, such as——"

Roberta came close to the bed and looked down at him, tired eyes suddenly bright with annoyance.

"Don't say it," she said. "If you are going to continue dealing in personalities and acting like a small boy, I shall ask to be transferred to some other case—one who will at least try to co-operate." Her voice softened. "Why can't you be good, Chris? I want to help you back to health. Why won't you go along with me?"

Chris gulped. Drops of sweat gathered on brow and upper lip. He tossed the bedclothes back from his shoulders while his blue eyes begged her to have patience with him. Almost immediately a chill shook him until his teeth chattered and Roberta tucked the blankets about him once more. She made an additional note on his chart, then turned back to the bed.

"I know," she whispered. "Don't mind anything I may have said, Chris. I've been touchy, too, but it won't happen again."

"You can be just as touchy as you want to," he muttered as the chill receded, leaving him pale and weak. "You're tops, Robin, and be sure to come back early. I'll try to endure Aunt Sadie —— Oh, who have we here? Thank God!"

The door had opened and, instead of Austin, Rhoda Deland entered looking like an angel in her immaculate uniform and serene morning freshness. Roberta at once felt disheveled and haggard. Deland picked up the chart after a brief "good morning" and Roberta had a sudden sharp desire to snatch it away from her. Instead she made a few remarks regarding the patient's progress and a suggestion as to his diet, and left the room.

She wondered who was responsible for the change. She didn't have long to wonder, however. Cynthia, with her nose for news, took time out to acquaint her with the latest developments. She had talked with Austin who had, quite without warning, been assigned to Forsyth, Garsden's mayor.

"The Forsyth family demanded her because of her remarkable record. That's the story and we are stuck with it; but you know, of course, Jitney operated last night—claimed it was an emergency. The funny thing is, Doc Jackson from Corinth General is supposed to be pinch-hitting for the chief while he's away. It seems Lewis was all for getting Jackson but Jitney informed him he was the man of the hour and would do what surgery was to be done while his uncle was away. Get that? 'His uncle.' The chief has been treating His Honor, who's an old crony, over a period of years for attacks of indigestion that come on after the City Fathers indulge in one of their banquets. They dined— too well—night before last. Hence the internal com- bustion. Lewis and Deland assisted Jitney and the operation came off as per his nibs' schedule. I tried to pump the circulating nurse but all she would say was that if that was an *emergency* appendectomy she was a striped baboon. But Jitney's sure swaggering about the place as if he had just performed a miracle. And

His Honor's a darned sick man today. However, the super-nurse will pull him through—I hope. Inasmuch as the chief's away, Jitney becomes important and proceeds to shift us about to suit himself. As a reward for backing him up regarding that *emergency* last night—Deland gets nephew. Morrison is fit to be tied and Lewis looks grim and has nothing to say. It's all a mess. Just makes me surer something is going on in this hospital. What sort of a guy is this nephew?"

"Splendid, Cyn," Roberta replied, only half listening to the other's enlightening conversation. "He's peevish and uncomfortable part of the time of course; but Chris is normally a darling."

"Chris? Darling? Is this fast work, Bob, or have you met before in some previous incarnation?"

"I met him two years ago. It was just before he left for South America. I thought he was one of the finest men I had ever known. I had no idea he was Holmes' nephew and was surprised when I found he was here in the hospital."

"Well, my girl, if there are any faint stirrings in that adamantine heart of yours over this Chris, for Pete's sake move fast, for sure as shooting Deland'll get to work on him and he'll go head-over-heels for her madonna looks and womanly graces—if any. I know men and I know they're putty in the hands of a clever woman. Deland is just about the cleverest there is in this joint."

"Thanks!" Roberta said shortly. "You're not very flattering to your friends."

"Oh-oh!" Cynthia soothed, an impish grin on her mischievous face. "But your cleverness doesn't run in the same direction, darling. Your worst enemy wouldn't accuse you of being a man-eater and your best friend couldn't say you know the faintest rudiments of acquisition. I take it you like this—this Chris in 217? Maybe he's the man—the heart interest you so sorely need."

"Don't talk nonsense!" Roberta snapped. "We are just good friends. I don't imagine Deland will get far with him. I mean, of course, in turning his head."

"You don't know that gal, darling," Cynthia insisted. "She's poison. She's got Jitney in the hollow of her hand. I don't know about Holmes. I haven't looked into that angle very closely and I must. Holmes is a widower and an eligible one at that in spite of his being sixty-ish."

"For Pete's sake get out of here and let me sleep," Roberta begged. "I'm sorry, Cyn," she hastened to add as she saw the sudden hurt in the other's eyes. "You ought to be in bed yourself instead of wandering about talking. Morning sleep is the best, you know very well, and about all we get in this boiler factory."

"Okay!" Cynthia said as she turned to go, but she couldn't resist a parting shot. "Irritation is one of the first symptoms. I'm relieved to see it."

If Roberta heard she didn't reply, and the door closed

with surprising quietness—for Cynthia. Roberta tossed
about on her narrow bed, her thoughts chaotic. Why
did Stan persist in tormenting her—in tempting her to
follow the dictates of heart rather than conscience?
She wondered if her face betrayed her to Chris's prob-
ing eyes. She wondered, too, why Chris disliked Stan.
Was it because he surmised Stan did not love his wife?
What a mess if he found out that Stan loved her!
Chris had urged her to keep the ring until he asked
for it. It would be a link between them—would make
her think of him. She didn't need the ring to do that.
She thought of him often, especially since the Tildons
had reappeared.

She got out of bed and went to her dressing table.
She kept the ring in an unused purse there, well hidden
beneath an assortment of handkerchiefs and scarfs. It
was safe. She examined it again. So plain because Chris
disliked "flossiness." Well, Deland was anything but
"flossy." Would he fall for Deland? She slipped the
ring on the third finger of her left hand and held it
up to the light. The sound of approaching footsteps
made her snatch it off and drop it back into its hiding
place. The footsteps paused for a moment then passed
on.

Roberta crept back to bed, thoroughly chilled, and
feeling like a silly schoolgirl. Well, even Chris wouldn't
accuse her of "flossiness." When at last she slept, her
lips were smiling.

When Roberta returned to 217 at seven that evening, she found the patient apparently improved. At least, he seemed serene enough. Deland turned at her entrance.

"I am sure you will experience no difficulty tonight, Cameron," she said in her cool, impersonal voice. "Doctor Nichols says the patient must have no excitement. I have exchanged the book you were reading him for another—one with less action."

Roberta bit back an angry retort. "I'm sure you mean to be helpful," she murmured with equal coolness, while seething inwardly. "I wasn't aware Doctor Nichols was the physician on this case."

"It would scarcely be anyone else," Deland said as she prepared to leave. "Good night, Mr. Baxter. See you in the morning. Please try not to undo what has been accomplished during the day."

Roberta kept her back to the room until she could control her anger. How dared she speak so to her! What a fool she was to think Deland could be treated like the other nurses! One had to be as coldly disdainful as she was. Meet ice with ice. She thought of all the sharp retorts she could have made and decided she was being petty. What did she care for Deland's opinion? Doctor Holmes had assigned her to this position because he felt sure she was capable of handling it. Deland had no authority over her and she intended letting her know it when that young lady came on duty at seven tomorrow morning. She laid down the chart and turned to meet the twinkling gaze from the man on the bed.

"Beautiful, isn't she?" he said with enthusiasm. "So she's the gal who's assigned to cheer my daylight hours and prepare me for the dark lonesomeness of the night. Stan tells me she's his favorite nurse. I can well believe it, and not in quite the way he intended I should. What a curse beauty can be—in some people! Well, Robin, how did you sleep this lovely spring day?" His voice was teasing.

"Very well, thank you. And you?"

"Oh, I didn't sleep—much. How could I with Madonna of the Snows ministering to me? I tell you, Robin, I never dreamed Uncle Doc was such a connoisseur. I'll have to keep tabs on the old boy. Can't be having him lose his head at his age."

"The doctor was in today?"

"If you mean dear Stanley? Yes. I suggested having Lewis drop in; but Doctor Nichols pooh-poohed the idea. He'll take care of me. You should have seen them together—I mean nurse and doctor. I was sure glad Stan is out of the running. Not even a Chinaman's chance for me if he wasn't. Don't you think she's beautiful, Robin?"

"Very beautiful," Roberta replied.

Chris was very docile. Unnaturally so, Roberta thought and wondered, miserably, if Rhoda Deland really impressed him as much as she seemed to. She picked up the book the day nurse had left and prepared to read aloud. Chris closed his eyes and snored realistically. She returned the book to the table, none too gently. Stanley Nichols appeared soon after eleven. He glanced at the chart and asked Chris a few questions, then motioned Roberta from the room. She stubbornly appeared to misunderstand and he paused in the doorway and said:

"Oh, Cameron, I want a word with you."

Chris yawned widely and murmured:

"Run along, little nursie. Don't you hear him calling, Robin dear?"

Roberta glared at him and left the room. "Well?" she asked as she had the night before. "What now?"

"Why the chip, Berta?" Stanley Nichols asked. "Chris riding you pretty hard? I have a theory it's bad policy to assign a nurse to a case if the two are known to each other. It is much better that a stranger takes charge. The patient is far more apt to co-operate and it is infinitely better for the morale of the nurse. I am going to see about making a change in this instance."

"Mr. Baxter is a model patient," Roberta said coolly. "I am sure any nurse assigned to him would agree. But, of course, it is for Doctor Holmes or Miss Morrison to say. It doesn't matter to me where I work. Certainly I did not ask for this case, Doctor Nichols."

"What's the matter, Berta? Has something happened to disturb you?" he asked solicitously.

"Nothing, Doctor."

He caught her hands in his, unmindful of possible interruptions, and whispered:

"You're unhappy, darling. So am I. I'll see you're put on day work ——" He started guiltily and dropped her hands. His face changed as if a veil had descended over it.

"I wanted to ask you something, Doctor," Deland's low, even voice broke in. She was wearing an evening gown under her fur wrap. Her beauty was startling. She glanced sharply at Roberta whose cheeks blazed with color, much to her annoyance. "It is about Mr. Baxter's taste in books. I don't approve of exciting yarns in his present condition ——"

Roberta escaped to her patient. Before the door closed, however, she heard Stan say:

"What's the idea?" and the tone he used wasn't that of a doctor to his favorite nurse. He sounded annoyed.

"So it's another pretty face ——" How did Deland dare use that tone to Stan? Roberta shut the door, standing for a moment with her back against it. She was bewildered. What was going on here? Did Cynthia have a real basis for the mystery she claimed existed?

Chris was watching her curiously. "What's the matter, Robin?" he asked. "Doctor bawl you out for not giving me the dope he left? Don't mind him, darling. He's too big for his britches."

"It wasn't Doctor Nichols. It was your day nurse— the lady you admire so extravagantly. She objects to your taste in books—or was it my taste she objected to?" Roberta knew she sounded catty but couldn't seem to help it. Just who was this Deland that she could be so authoritative and get away with it? Was Cynthia right in thinking she and Stan had known each other before she came here? And was she attempting to oust Morrison? Was Stan the attraction that had brought her from New York to Garsden? And just what was she to him, anyway?

"Open the door, Robin," Chris demanded suddenly. "I like to feel hospitable. The open door! Sounds like an international project, doesn't it?"

Roberta pretended not to have heard the request. How could she open the door when Stan and Deland might be still standing just outside?

"Look, Robin, if you don't open that door I shall get right out of bed and do it myself." Chris spoke decidedly. Roberta wondered what he suspected.

"But, Chris, I can't—you can't. It would look like spying—like ——" she stammered.

"Why should it?" he demanded. "Why should I or anyone wish to spy on Nichols or, for that matter, on my lovely day nurse? I ask you. Open the door. One, two——"

Roberta turned the handle and the door slowly swung back. She was behind it and heard the tap, tap, tapping of high heels receding down the dim corridor. She breathed a sigh of relief. At least she hadn't overheard anything.

"You are a badly spoiled young man," she scolded in her sudden reaction. "Do you always get your own way?"

"Quite frequently," he grinned up at her. "When I don't it's because it's best I shouldn't. I wonder just why our beautiful madonna shows such flattering interest in me, Robin. Don't answer. I can see your disapproval. But to think of her coming over here when she could and should have been resting, just to see I don't get unduly excited! It—it's really quite touching—don't you think? How did she look, Robin? Beautiful as ever?"

"More beautiful," Roberta said. "She was evidently returning from a big evening. She was dressed accordingly. You really should have seen her, Chris."

Chris grinned slyly, then said with what sounded like jealousy: "Out with some blasted interne, I suppose. Fickle—all of you. Where's the book you started reading to me before Nichols appeared? Hand it over," he ordered.

Roberta gave him the book and he shoved it under the mattress of his bed.

"Find a good murder mystery, Robin. I feel just like

listening to an account of how people get rid of their pet hates."

Robin laughed and felt infinitely better. "Don't you feel at all sleepy, Chris?" she asked. He shook his head.

"Never was more wide awake in my life," he insisted. "Let's talk."

"All right. Tell me about your childhood and your bridge building in South America."

"Oh, my childhood is summed up in a few words, Robin. It was so darned carefree and happy that it just doesn't make much of a story. As for the engineering—most of that is hard work, bad weather and hunger for someone of my own kind to talk to. That's when I wrote you all those letters I didn't mail. On that last job we fought insects, humidity and labor trouble. We bucked ignorance, stupidity and superstition; but we won out. The bridge is done and stands a monument to American enterprise and cheap labor."

"Do you like bridge building, Chris? In far corners of the world?" she asked, sensing his need to talk.

"Listen to the girl! Do I like doing a man's work in the world? Do I like seeing my dream take concrete shape before my eyes? Do I like hearing the chief say: 'Well done, Baxter. We're proud of that job.' What do you think, Robin?"

Roberta's eyes shone. "You love it, don't you? I was sure you did. How could Gail have let you go

[223]

down there alone? You could have had such fun together ——"

"Not Gail," Chris said without rancor. "Do you know what it means to live in a construction camp, Robin? No luxuries and mighty few comforts. No rugs on the rough unpainted floors of the two-room shack in which a couple of cots and maybe a chair or two, a table and an oil stove comprise the furniture. No communication with the outside world except on mail days which is once in two or three weeks or whenever the nearest town gets around to delivering it. None of your own kind—except your small staff of assistants who are quite apt to get drunk or quit because of loneliness or homesickness—within two or three hundred miles—but Lord, what scenery! What stories the natives tell of a civilization lost these many centuries! What fishing on one's day off! What—what—bugs!" He grinned sheepishly. "You think I'm nuts, don't you?" he asked. "But I love it—anywhere away from the fuss and restrictions of modern living. I own a ranch in Montana and if a certain prospective job in Manila fizzles out as it undoubtedly will under this present chaos, I'm going out there and run it myself. I have a good manager but if some of my dreams come true, I think I'll settle down and become a rancher. I have a notion you would love it, Robin. I'm not so sure about Mati Hari."

"Mati Hari?" Roberta asked, puzzled.

[224]

"The lady who deigns to be my day nurse. Doesn't she make you think of her? I mean, she's mysterious and intriguing."

"It's just the metropolitan training, my dear Chris," Roberta assured him. "Cyn says it's due to having a straight nose and an eccentric hair-do."

"Sin? Who is she or is it a he? The person sounds perspicacious. Is that the real name?"

"Cyn—with a C. Her name is Cynthia. She fancies herself as a detective and is always looking for clues. She's funny and sweet and very, very clever." Roberta spoke enthusiastically.

"A nurse in Rebecca Moore?" and at Roberta's nod of assent, "I must make a note of that. I must meet Cyn."

"I'll guarantee you will if you remain here long enough. Cyn has a way of meeting people. I wish she was your day nurse—you'd be entertained—beautifully."

"But I am entertained, my dear," Chris told her. "I find the present incumbent vastly enlightening. You know, I'm somewhat like your friend Cynthia—I love a mystery and I find it most amusing to ferret out dark and hidden secrets and expose the villain in all his knavery. I should imagine a hospital was a swell place for intrigue and villainy to hold forth. You have all sorts of people here and——"

"Don't let your imagination run away with you,"

Roberta warned. "Rebecca Moore Memorial is just about the quietest, staidest, most conservative establishment in the world. Babies are born and occasionally people die—quite naturally, I assure you. Some patients come for operations—most of which are successful, and others suffering from the various other ills that man is heir to. But everything is in the regular run of the mill. Not once, since my advent, has anything especially spectacular happened. People come here for help and they usually get it. That's what hospitals are for. Rebecca Moore is no exception. The only thing in which we excel is in having Doctor Holmes as chief of staff. That is a boon to Garsden and the county."

"Uncle Doc's great, I know," Chris conceded, "but just the same I'm going to do a bit of sleuthing while I'm here. Maybe I can uncover a mystery or something."

"I hate snooping," Roberta said sharply. "If a person has a mystery in his life he usually wants to keep it secret. Why should anyone want to dig up something that can't possibly concern him?"

"But it might concern him. That's the point," Chris insisted. "Why, that's how newspapers are run—by reporters rushing in where angels fear to tread. It would be a drab world indeed without those curious ones who ferret out interesting and intriguing facts about their fellows. I don't mean scandal, my dear

Roberta. For shame! That's what you were thinking, now wasn't it? How could you! Who within these sacred portals ever does anything scandalous? Echo answers—'Who-o-oo?'"

"Perhaps not actually scandalous—only having the appearance. Take that perfectly harmless episode in my own spotless past—the time I sought shelter in a lakeside cottage. Remember how, by telling several whopping falsehoods, you thought to avert gossip and succeeded only in painting in a background of intrigue to an entirely innocent escapade? Suppose someone ferreted that out. Where would you—where would we both be? I have just begun to breathe easy again after the Tildons dropped from oblivion to give a fillip to the muddle I supposed was dead and forgotten. You see, Chris, one can never be sure about such things." Roberta spoke earnestly.

"Well, if the worst happens, you have a wedding ring in your possession and you can feel pretty sure I'll always be ready to make an honest—man of myself." He laughed at her sudden stiffening. "You thought I was going to say 'an honest woman of you,' didn't you? But just the same, the promise holds—if my sins catch up with me."

"Don't worry," Roberta retorted loftily. "It will never be necessary. *I* can promise *you*."

"Maybe not necessary, exactly, but—expedient, shall we say?" His eyes were quizzical. "Don't be so prickly,

Robin. Suppose I do decide to carry you off to my ranch, I assure you it will be done quite legally——"

"Don't talk nonsense," she interrupted, but her lips were smiling. "Sometimes I feel sure the infection must have gone to your head," she told him.

Chapter 19

PAULA WINSLOW'S NAME CREPT INTO THE CONVERSATION
next afternoon when a group of nurses rested in the
gymnasium after a fast game of basketball.

"I heard she haunts Doc's office," one girl con-
tributed. "I know they go riding together because my
brother met them 'way out Beach Tree Road one
afternoon last week. He had to stop his truck until
their horses passed. What does he see in her?"

"Money, my child," another nurse offered. "She
may have been a beauty once but she certainly isn't
now."

"It's her line, my frans," a third girl said. "And she
has her points, too. Some people admire even a slat if
it happens to serve as an entree into the sanctums of
the elite. In his case, though, I can't see the necessity.
His wife's a thoroughbred even if she did slip badly
when she took him on. I heard his real name is Nicoli

and he changed it to Nichols when he started on the road to success."

Roberta walked away. She hated gossip and refused to have any part in it. Cynthia caught her arm.

"Wait for me," she said. "I'm sorry if your sensibilities are shocked at the free discussion of our handsome Jitney's irregularities, Bob, but if he doesn't watch his step he's going to come a cropper. This isn't New York where a person can get away with anything without causing comment or censure and he ought to have sense enough to know it. What with being mixed up with Winslow and Deland and who knows how many others—he's sitting on a volcano and I don't mean maybe. That Winslow dame is crazy as a loon and how she manages to keep out of trouble is a mystery to me."

"Listen, Cynthia," Roberta said coldly. "It is none of our business what she does. And if Doctor Nichols is friendly with her, that, too, is none of our business. I refuse to take any part in this apparent campaign to disqualify him——"

"Oh, so you heard that, did you?" Cynthia asked. "And do you mean to say you approve of his political maneuvers among the goofy members of the Board—his and Deland's?"

"I don't know anything about any maneuvers——" Roberta began.

"Then it's about time you did," Cynthia retorted.

"I only know that if Doctor Holmes has decided he is capable and efficient, he no doubt is. If you people are thinking he wants to come to Rebecca Moore as Assistant Surgeon, I'm sure you are mistaken. His job with Doctor Wharton promises a splendid future. I doubt if he has had much surgical experience. At least I——"

"You speak as if you were on friendly terms with him, Bob," Cynthia said. "His card reads 'Physician *and* Surgeon,' darling."

"Why shouldn't I be?" Roberta asked. "I know of no reason why I should be anything but friendly."

"Honestly, Bob, there are times when I think you're positively deaf, dumb and blind, especially dumb," Cynthia said in exasperation. They had reached Roberta's room and Cynthia threw herself into the nearest chair as if exhausted. "Listen, Bob," she said slowly and clearly as if trying to instruct a particularly stupid child. "He's wormed his way into the good graces of the Board's two most influential women—Mrs. Foster and Miss Whitcomb—both old fossils and relatives of the Winslow gal. Deland brought a letter of introduction to them from Massy—seems she was his head nurse or superintendent in the ritzy hospital he had. That's who Jitney was with before he came here, you know, or didn't you? Anyway, there's a plot afoot to bring about changes in Rebecca Moore. While the chief's away seems to be a good time to do some heavy

[231]

electioneering. There's dirty work going on at the crossroads and you'd better get wise to yourself. And Nichols *is* a surgeon, Bob, at least he claims to be. He did what surgery, if any, was done in Massy's select hospital. He certainly wants the job here. So remember—preparedness is the watchword." She got to her feet and strolled toward the door.

" Some of the rest of us are doing a bit of campaigning on the q.t. And it may surprise the invaders to discover they are not to have everything their own way. Two can play at their game. Sorry to insist the ' gift from heaven ' has a clay foot, darling, but such seems to be the case. As for Deland—I bet my best slip she's out of here come Michaelmas, whenever that is. 'Bye, Bobby. Keep your fingers crossed."

Roberta sat staring into space for a long moment after the door had closed on Cynthia. Of course a lot of what she had said was purest nonsense. Cynthia dramatized everything. She didn't like either Stan or Deland and consequently their most innocent actions were painted in glaring colors.

Stan was being very foolish. Roberta didn't believe for one moment there was anything wrong in his association with either Deland or any of his patients. It was quite understandable that women should make fools of themselves over him—hadn't she been in danger of doing so herself? She knew a sudden sense of relief—of escape, that came as a distinct shock. She found she could think of Stan dispassionately. Ever since her meeting with Sylvia, her mental attitude toward him had changed. She thought of him now as the husband of her new friend, Sylvia Nichols.

She wondered about Paula Winslow. Had she quite recovered from her illness? She intended inquiring of Doctor Lewis when next she saw him. The opportunity came almost at once for she and the resident met outside the door of 217 that same evening. The doctor frowned when Roberta asked him how Mrs. Winslow was coming along.

" Has she quite recovered, Doctor? "

" No. She has not recovered," he said. " In fact, I think she is in bad shape; but try to make her do anything she doesn't want to. Her father has begged, her mother wept and I have warned. We might just as well hold our breath. Some day she'll crack or I'm no diagnostician."

" I'm sorry," Roberta murmured. " She could so easily be an attractive girl. Was—do you suppose she still loves her husband, Doctor? Might not that be a contributory cause? "

" I thought of that; but I'm afraid not. She's a predatory youngster—has always yearned for something she couldn't have. She delights in rousing jealousy among her girl friends. Seems to thrive on it. The boy she married was engaged to another girl—her closest friend at the time. I don't know, Cameron," he

went on worriedly, "Pauline used to be a cute kid——
Maybe that's the trouble now. What was cute at five
is decidedly obnoxious at twenty. I don't believe in
corporal punishment as a general thing; but I certainly
would enjoy taking Pauline across my knee and getting
in some good lusty whacks with my slipper. At that,
it might be too late now. The thing I'm afraid of is
she'll do some real damage before she's through."

"Damage—you mean to herself, Doctor?"

"No. I mean to others. Oh, I don't mean bodily
harm—though that isn't impossible. I mean—but I've
talked too much as it is. Forget it, Cameron. How's
your patient? I wish we had you over in K right
now. Eleven influenza cases, three pleurisy and one
strep. That strep case must be moved at once. I don't
care if the family is on relief. She's going into a
private room if I have to pay for it out of my own
pocket."

Roberta knew he was talking more to himself than
to her. He had probably already forgotten her existence.
The resident took his work seriously—was really a
slave to the hospital. Well, he had given it twenty-five
years of his best endeavor so what was one to expect?
The story went that Stan considered he had outlived
his usefulness. He was in favor of a younger man. Yet
none of the staff thought of Doctor Lewis as old. He
was sixty, perhaps; lean, spry and alert as a man half
his age. Roberta hoped the chief wouldn't listen to

Doctor Nichols. They all loved Doctor Lewis—nurses and patients alike.

Shaking his head, the resident hurried away and Roberta prepared to enter 217. Doctor Nichols was with Chris and Roberta thought they looked as if they had been having a heated discussion. Deland was nowhere in sight. How dared she leave before the night relief arrived? But maybe Stan had dismissed her.

"That's the way it is," Stan said and left the room without a glance at her.

"So you want to quit your job with me, do you? Running out on me again," Chris said after a moment in which he studied her face with critical unfriendly eyes.

"Running out? Quitting? I don't know what you mean." Roberta was startled. The hospital seemed to have suddenly gone crazy.

"Oh, I don't suppose you actually asked to be relieved," he went on, "but I understand you prefer one of the wards or perhaps someone you don't know. Nichols doesn't approve of our being together, it seems, so I'm to have still another nurse. Say, what's the matter with me, anyway?"

"Ask, rather, what's the matter with the hospital?" Roberta countered. "I never heard of such queer goings-on in my life. This is all news to me, but of course I shall go where I am sent. That is the rule of the hospital." She spoke stiffly.

"Just what authority has Stan Nichols in this hospital?" Chris persisted. "He's merely one of the staff of consulting physicians, isn't he? And that only as Doc Wharton's substitute. I wish Uncle Doc didn't have to stay the whole ten days at that blasted convention. There's something queer going on here."

"Do you see it, too?" she asked, but not aloud. Instead, she smiled and said: "Don't imagine things." She was puzzled at the situation. She felt Chris's eyes on her. He seemed to have changed since she left him this morning.

"Mati Hari doesn't seem to be very popular with the nurses, does she?" he asked tentatively, after a moment.

"I'm sure I don't know," Roberta answered.

"Probably jealousy. She's beautiful, all right, and gives a lot of indirect information. I've had one or two eye-openers already. It will be interesting to watch developments. How true it is all humans both male and female are fallible where beauty is concerned."

"So I have heard."

"Do you know, Cameron, I think I shall make arrangements to leave here—go out to my sister's in Spokane. I could hop a plane and be there in a few hours."

Roberta was startled. "Cameron." He had never called her anything but Robin. She bit her lip, determined not to let it bother her.

"I doubt if that would be wise," she said reasonably.

"Wise? Perhaps wiser than lying here watching events develop—knowing myself powerless to prevent a tragedy," he muttered savagely.

Roberta turned and looked down at him. His face was flushed, his eyes held an angry light. She reached for her thermometer and he turned his head.

"Take that cursed thing away!" he ordered.

"Under your tongue, please," she soothed, her fingers on his pulse. "Just what happened?" she asked after a minute as she shook down the mercury. Apparently this was genuine anger for his temperature was almost normal.

"Oh, nothing—everything," he growled. "Just what do *you* want?" he snapped, as Ambers, one of the older nurses, came into the room.

"Doctor Lewis wants you in K, Cameron," she said, her voice controlled but her eyes blazing. Then, under her breath, she muttered: "I wish Doctor Holmes would come back where he belongs. That Deland's pulling some fast ones."

Roberta stared at her in amazed consternation. "I don't understand," she said.

"You will—in time," the older woman replied. "But maybe some of the rest of us can get in a few licks."

Chris was watching—trying to understand the low-toned conversation. He lay with his hands behind his head, one knee making a tent of the bedclothes.

"I must be very dumb," Roberta said. "How can Deland do anything—she's just a nurse——"

"She'll be superintendent if the wires she's pulling don't snap back in her face. She's got some of the trustees eating out of her hand already and Nichols is backing her. They say Morrison and Lewis are past their usefulness. Just what is she to him, anyway? Tell me that."

"I wish you'd either speak louder or shut up," Chris growled. "Or am I supposed to be deaf, as well as dumb?"

Roberta turned and left the room without a word. Not even stopping when he called to her. She was upset and angry. Just what was going on in Rebecca Moore? And just who was this Rhoda Deland? Was it true that she and Stan were old friends? Was it he who was responsible for her coming here? Morrison and Lewis—it was unthinkable they should be let out. Why, they were as much a part of Rebecca Moore as was the chief himself.

The evening visiting hours were in full swing and as she walked through the corridor, she was greeted from time to time by callers but she answered automatically, quite unaware of their identity. She reached ward K and found the resident and Davis, a junior nurse, in attendance. Doctor Lewis eyed her for a moment then smiled.

"Seems to be some rapid-fire changes going on here

just now," he said quizzically. "But as long as I'm the gainer, I'm not worried. I wanted you here in the first place but the chief was worried about his precious nephew and felt the best was none too good for him. Nichols, who considers he stands in the chief's place while he's away, thinks otherwise. Keep your fingers crossed, Cameron," he cautioned, "but your chin up. Things are going to happen." Here it was again.

"Tell me what it's all about, Doctor," Roberta begged.

"Can't, just now. But I put my oar in where I thought it would do the most good. I wired the chief to take a plane and get back here pronto. He should be here by midnight."

Roberta looked relieved. "Grand!" she whispered.

"The strep case is in 185. I had the devil of a time getting her in there, but I did. Got Cooper on it, too. She's a fighter and I need a few fighters just now."

"I wish I knew what it's all about," Roberta protested.

"You will," he promised and hurried away.

For the remainder of that night, Roberta was far too busy to spend much time in conjecture. With the midnight sandwiches and coffee, she listened to more grumbling. Word had gone around that Morrison was resigning under pressure, and that the resident was to be replaced by a younger doctor. Someone had said Nichols was coming in as assistant surgeon and the orderlies and internes were calling for bets he would be chief within a year.

"Oh, that can't possibly be, Davis!" Roberta protested when she heard. "Why, Holmes is his wife's uncle. He gave him his chance here. Anyway, he hasn't had the experience—he couldn't hold the job."

"Oh, Holmes is soft where his family is concerned. He'll probably back him up—do the work and Nichols'll have the name. I don't know how Nichols is going to work it, but that's the talk."

"Nonsense!" Roberta felt it was a lot of silly gossip.

"And another thing," Davis went on belligerently, "when that Deland gets to be superintendent, I get out. I wouldn't work under her one single minute. I bet ninety percent of the staff will walk out with me, too."

"I think you're all crazy," Roberta said. "Deland wouldn't qualify for that job. She's too young for one thing and lacks the proper training——"

"Oh, she's not so young," Davis persisted. "She's close to thirty, if she's a day. And she claims to have a degree from Columbia and another from some place in Philadelphia. That's what *she* says. She was superintendent of a small private hospital somewhere near New York before she came here."

Roberta was silent for a long moment. It did look queer her coming here so soon after Stan's arrival. She shook her head emphatically. Of course it was all just coincidence. Everyone was jittery because the chief was away. Roberta was glad he was returning, for she never doubted he would come as soon as he received Lewis' wire.

She went off duty at seven. The day nurses were tight-lipped and uncommunicative. Her eyes questioned them but they shook their heads. At the breakfast table she felt the underground rumblings of the threatened eruption. No one had much to say. Even Cynthia was silent and watchful. Roberta went to her room, undressed and slipped into bed. She thought Cynthia would come in but she didn't and at last she fell into the heavy sleep of exhaustion.

It was after two when she awoke. Footsteps came down the hall and paused at her door. The handle turned cautiously and Cynthia poked her head in.

"Awake?" she asked superfluously. "The chief's back, Bob, and are we glad! It was certainly a pleasant surprise when he walked into 185 at a little after one to look at our strep case. Lewis was with him and Holmes complimented him on moving her into a private room. Gee, Bob, he's a grand old boy!"

"Tell me what's going on, Cyn," Roberta demanded, sitting up in bed, arms about her knees. Her curly hair was a nimbus about her flushed face and her eyes were bright with curiosity.

"I don't know what's at the bottom of it even yet; but I can put two and two together and make as many as Deland and Jitney can. It seems Deland has her eye on Morrison's job. I'll bet a dollar to a fresh doughnut Jitney promised it to her when he came here. Being the fair-haired boy, so to speak, he thought he could accomplish anything he set his heart on. I know he slated Lewis for the dustheap. But from all my observation, Lewis isn't worried about his job. What seems to worry him is Nichols getting to be assistant surgeon —he insists he isn't qualified."

"With Holmes' help, maybe he is," Roberta said, but without conviction. She bore Stan no ill will. She just felt he wasn't big enough for the job. But she recalled the Board was three-fourths female.

Cynthia shook her head. "He lacks what it takes, Bob," she insisted. "How old is the chief? Sixty, would you say?"

"I imagine so," Roberta said. "He is getting on in years and with training it would be perfectly logical, I suppose, for Doctor Nichols to take his place."

"You're hopeless, Bob," the other said despairingly. "How can you stand up for him? If I didn't know you, I'd fear you had fallen for him—hard, like a lot of other females; but not you. You're too level-headed and—and decent. I heard something—I wasn't supposed to either, but I have keen hearing, you know. Just before I went off duty this morning, the chief and Doc Murdock stopped to see how 185 was reacting to that new serum and I heard Holmes tell him he had located his assistant. You know, Murdock's mother is on the Board. He's a terrible Miss Nancy and he gives me the creeps; but I will say that he is wonderful to the charity cases in this hospital; but of course he can afford to—with his money. He's especially interested in the performance of sulfanilamide and sulfapyridine. Well, to get back to my story: he asked where on earth Holmes had discovered him when so many medical students are going in for specialized medicine and so few taking up surgery."

"Well?" Roberta prodded impatiently.

"He didn't mention his name, but said he had had a year at the Mayo clinic and was highly recommended. Nichols didn't go to the Mayo clinic, did he? I was under the impression he did two years interning in New York and got married almost at once. I haven't said a word of this to anyone but you, Bob, because I was not supposed to hear it and, anyway, I thought it might be the chief was giving Murdock the run-around knowing the Board is after him to get an assistant. He's been promising for the past five years and since old man Moore passed on, I guess they've been growing even more insistent."

"How about Morrison? Has she resigned?"

"I don't think so—yet. Granted she is sort of old-fashioned; we all love her and she runs this place as smoothly as if it was greased—which it is, I guess, with her simple kindliness and understanding. I doubt if anyone could have better discipline than Morrison gets by just not demanding the unreasonable. We're on our honor to do the right thing and somehow we do it. I think it would be a shame to can her. I know Jitney treats her like dirt—the rat! Deland finds her amusing. I could slap her down with the keenest pleasure. Oh, and I did hear that never since Morrison's advent has Rebecca Moore been in the red. She's not only a good superintendent and manager, but a financial wizard as well. The Board's crazy if it lets her go. But come on, Bob. Let's go for a walk. Right now this place smothers me. Let's get out."

"Okay," Roberta said. "I'll meet you outside in twenty minutes." Could Stan win the approval of the Board to his plans? She hoped not.

Chapter 20

THE ATMOSPHERE OF REBECCA MOORE MEMORIAL Hospital smoldered for days. The chief went about the business of looking in on the various patients, performing operations as they came to hand, and carrying on the work of the small but busy hospital with his usual gruff efficiency.

Roberta saw little of Doctor Nichols after she was changed to day duty in Ward K. And though he sometimes accompanied Doctor Holmes and the resident on their rounds, which was in itself an innovation, she maintained an attitude of impersonal aloofness that precluded any attempt at friendliness on his part. The chief and he talked over the various cases, conferring over charts and referring occasionally to her or to Miss Morrison. Doctor Lewis seemed to stay in the background.

On one occasion, however, Doctor Lewis was absent and Doctor Nichols seemed determined to get her alone. The day was warm and the ward bright with sunshine. Everyone appeared on the gain and Roberta felt relieved that the annual siege of flu, measles and other ills of late spring was about over. The three passed down the ward and Roberta wondered what had become of the resident. Was it true that Lewis was to be removed? She stole a glance at the superintendent. Her eyes were on the chief. Never by word or glance did she acknowledge the presence of Doctor Nichols. If he spoke to her directly, she answered, but so coolly and impersonally that Roberta marveled at his accepting it without comment. Once she saw him glare malevolently when the unexpectedly impressive superintendent bluntly dubbed one of his suggestions impracticable in a hospital the size of Rebecca Moore. What had gotten into him? He was changed. She saw the chief lift shaggy brows in a questioning glance and was glad Miss Morrison stood her ground.

He paused beside Roberta as she stood at the small desk just outside the door.

"Everything okay?" he asked, genially. "Baxter's much better. In fact, we're going to let him go up to the solarium a little while every day, weather permitting. He'll be about on crutches in no time at all. Coddling isn't good for a man of his type. He thinks he will be able to leave for Washington next week. It won't be a hard trip by plane. Do him good. Be right with you, Doctor," he called.

Doctor Holmes had returned and stood waiting near the elevator.

"I'll see you later, Berta," Stan whispered. "I've got to talk to you. Things are waking up in this old mausoleum. It will be better for us all—or most of us. Can you get down to Receiving at four for a few minutes? Coming!" he muttered as the chief took a few steps toward them. He was frowning and Roberta knew he was not pleased at the delay.

She didn't answer Stan's question and with an angry imprecation he strode away.

Doctor Lewis had prescribed the solarium for two of the convalescing patients in K. Roberta wheeled them to the elevator and saw they were comfortable on the roof. The place was beginning to show signs of summer. Boxes were brilliant with color. Daffodils and tulips bloomed in profusion and the small fir trees and gay umbrellas made the whole place attractive.

She stood for a moment, looking out over the city. Lazy white clouds moved slowly across the wide expanse of blue. A faint warm breeze stirred her soft hair and she lifted her face to meet it. She leaned for a moment against one of the huge red chimneys and breathed deeply of the fresh spring air. She would have liked to be at Shandleys Beach right now. Or perhaps over at Pan's Haven where the hepaticas, trilliums and violets grew in such profusion. What fun she and Ginny used to have in early spring searching for the first mountain laurel! A feeling of nostalgia brought a lump to her throat and she turned to go downstairs, but stopped, completely paralyzed. In the protecting shadow of a clump of evergreens, two figures paused and merged as their lips met. Roberta shrank back but not before she had recognized them. She tried to hurry past as if she had seen nothing, but someone caught her hand.

"Hello, Robin!" a familiar voice whispered. "And you are the gal who assured me nothing ever happened here. Stick around, darling—you'll see plenty. I've missed you, Robin," he persisted, his fingers clinging to her lax hand.

She felt rather than saw Stan and Deland approaching and pulled her hand free.

"I'm so glad you are better." She smiled down, unseeing, at the man in the wheel chair.

"Better!" Chris muttered. "Fed up, rather." He glared malevolently after Doctor Nichols as he disappeared downstairs. Deland walked over to Chris and said in her cool authoritative voice:

"Time to go back. We must not overdo." She paid no attention to Roberta who lingered for a moment until Stan should have left the vicinity, and Chris said:

"What's the rush? I just got here. Am I supposed not to talk to my friends?"

"Friends? I wasn't aware you had friends here, Mr.

Baxter," Deland said, then as an afterthought: "Oh, yes. Of course, Cameron—but I understood—she's scarcely a friend—or is she—now?"

Chris ignored the implication.

"Good-bye, Robin," he called as Roberta sought the stairs.

"She seems in something of a hurry," Deland said smoothly. "Doctor Nichols left by the stairs, too, you'll notice." Her light laugh was significant.

"That isn't all I noticed," Chris muttered, but Deland didn't hear.

Stanley was waiting at the foot of the stairs when Roberta descended and she tried to pass without speaking, but he barred the way.

"What's the matter, Berta?" he asked, anxiously, catching her hand in his. "Have I done something to offend you? Surely you're not sore because I arranged to have you changed from Baxter to K? I thought you would appreciate I was thinking only of your personal feelings in the matter. I thought you certainly couldn't enjoy taking care of a man you knew——"

"Please, Doctor Nichols, I must get back to my patients."

"Your patients can wait for a few minutes I think," he said. "You've changed, Berta."

Roberta's head went back. She looked directly at him, her eyes enormous in her white face. "Yes. That's it. I have changed. I have recovered my senses. I don't even like you any more. I must have been crazy if I ever did." She wrenched her hand away and fled.

It was that very night the storm broke. The staff was at dinner when word of the new assistant's arrival swept the hospital. No one knew his name except that it wasn't Nichols. Cynthia caught Roberta's eye and winked. After dinner she disappeared and it was two hours later when she entered Roberta's room where that young lady was putting a finger wave in Clara Bowen's short black hair. Cynthia bounced into the room and flung herself on the bed.

"Well, gals, I've got all the dirt at last," she panted.

"Spill it, then," Clara suggested. Roberta said nothing, but went on with the job in hand.

"The new assistant surgeon is Rufus Stafford and he hails from Minnesota. The meeting of the Trustees was held this afternoon and approved the chief's choice unanimously. Also they refused to accept Morrison's tentative resignation, considering her an exceptional superintendent, and they raised Lewis' salary. Hurrah— three cheers for our side! Also, I understand, though this is not official, Jitney's name does not now appear on the staff of consulting physicians. How have the mighty fallen! Amen. I don't know what misfortune has befallen Deland—something, I hope. Anyway, her fangs are out—she can't do any more damage—here. The blitzkrieg has failed. Home sweet home remains to us as it was before the advent of the two who threatened to disrupt everything we hold sacred, or at least dear."

"I'm glad," was all Roberta said.

"Of course Jitney will always be under foot, more or less, I suppose," Cynthia went on, "but he won't be quite so cocky as he has been. How I have longed to tweak his classic nose when he has glared if I happened to see him doing something—unethical, shall we say? I knew he intended getting rid of me when he came into power. I'd like to give him the merry ha ha!"

"But how about all the political maneuvers you talked of?" Roberta asked, slipping a curl from the comb and pinning it in place. "They must have failed."

"I'll say they failed—100 percent. It seems Mrs. Winslow's old aunts or great-aunts, whichever they are, don't hold with this modern flippant attitude toward marriage and the home. It burned them up when Pauline or Paula divorced her husband but she started a holocaust when she got her hook into Jitney—a married man—another girl's husband and 'dear Doctor Holmes' niece' at that! They were shocked beyond words. Then, to add to the conflagration, word somehow reached them that our Miss Deland was very fond of the society of married men—preferably good-looking young doctors. Then the fat was in the fire with a vengeance. Such things could not be tolerated in Rebecca Moore. It was a distinct blot on the otherwise

[251]

stainless escutcheon of our beloved hospital, etc., etc. Anyway, Miss Deland has been requested to terminate her services at the end of the month. I'm not absolutely sure about that last, but it's quite in character. Maybe it's wishful thinking on my part; but I'm hoping it's true because I want her out of here before I leave."

"Leave?" Roberta cried. "Cynthia, are you and Homer getting married?"

At Cynthia's nod, she caught and held her close for a moment then kissed her softly.

"I'm so glad," she whispered.

"You see," Cynthia explained, her eyes bright, "Ma's going out to the Coast to live with her sister. It seems she's enjoying poor health and her husband—Homer says he's lousy with money—wants her to make her home with them permanently. I got a special delivery letter this afternoon just before dinner. I haven't told Morrison yet and I sort of dread it. She's been swell to me."

Clara gathered up comb and wave set and dashed for the door.

"We'll give you a shower, Cyn," she promised. "Can't stop to discuss plans now though. Got a heavy date. Thanks for the wave, Bob. Do something for you some time," and the door slammed.

"I'm so happy about you and Homer, Cyn," Roberta reiterated when Clara's footsteps had died away. "You're both so wonderful!"

"Applesauce!" Cynthia scoffed. "Though we do kind of like each other. But that news seems trivial beside the other. Have you seen either party of the first part lately, Bob? I mean since the Board meeting?"

Roberta shook her head.

"How's uncle's nephew coming along? I saw him and Deland in the elevator one afternoon. His expression said plainly that the fat canary he had just consumed was a most satisfying morsel. I couldn't repress a friendly grin and he grinned back. I have a notion her royal highness didn't approve. He looks nice, Bob, although I must say he'd never even in his palmiest days take a beauty prize—like—say, Jitney."

"I think Chris is wonderful looking, Cynthia Cooper," Roberta declared emphatically. "His face is strong and kind and clever. He's honorable and chivalrous and—and——"

"Spare me!" cried Cynthia. "Why, Bobby, you sound as if you liked the lad!"

"I do," Roberta said stoutly. "He's the most splendid man I know."

"Spoken like a lady, Cameron—spoken like a lady. Did you keep that luncheon set Mrs. Benson made you?"

Roberta laughed. "I forgot all about it. It's still in my trunk."

"Well, I'm glad your hope chest is at least started. Oh, Bob, I'm so terribly happy! I had begun to think it would never come off." Cynthia's eyes suddenly swam with tears and she dashed them angrily away. She hated obvious emotion at any time. "Can you imagine me being such a sap, Bob?"

Roberta had not called on Sylvia Nichols since that afternoon in April when she had been invited for tea. Sylvia had sent her messages on two different occasions but both times Roberta had been on day duty and unable to accept. She had been glad as she had no desire to encounter Stanley. She had only disgust for her naïve infatuation for him—for her gullibility.

As she thought back to that brief two weeks of nearly two years ago, she was practically certain Stanley Nichols had no real intention of breaking his engagement with Sylvia Bartlett. Sylvia represented security to him—a future—success in his profession—social prestige. All his protestations to the contrary, she, Roberta Cameron, was merely an incident, perhaps one of many such—the subject of a summer flirtation. Hot blood dyed her cheeks at the memory of her behavior—of her willingness to accept him at his face value. What a fool she had been! She wished she might never have to see him again, yet why not? He no longer meant anything to her. She was quite sure of that. But his very presence here in the hospital kept the memory of her humiliation fresh. She asked herself why it should. He was the one to be ashamed, for he had deliberately wooed her—broken down her defenses and extracted from her a confession of love.

"The best way to conquer a difficulty is to face it," her father had insisted, "for a battle faced is half won."

"I'll face it," she said resolutely, "and I defy it to get me down again." Her mirrored face startled her with its fierce determination and she laughed aloud. "How silly to be upset over a memory!"

Two days later, Roberta was back in 217. Apparently, Rhoda Deland had not waited until the end of the month but had left at once. At least, her room in the nurses' annex was vacant and she failed to report for duty the day after the Board meeting. Whether or not she had left Garsden was conjecture. No one cared particularly, for she had made no friends during her brief stay. It seemed to Roberta that the atmosphere of the hospital cleared with her departure. She was quite sure meals tasted better because of the general air of friendliness and good fellowship prevailing. That had been absent ever since the coming of Deland.

She hadn't seen Doctor Nichols since the Board meeting and supposed he was deliberately avoiding her. She found little sympathy in her heart for him.

Chapter 21

HALF PAST THREE, THIRTY MINUTES AFTER REGULAR hours and Doctor Stanley Nichols' office in the First National Bank Building had slowly emptied. Anna Hoxie, his office nurse, had gone to the drug store two blocks away. Doctor Nichols sat at his desk in an attitude of dejection. All his well-laid plans had gone haywire. He couldn't figure it out. Just what had happened? Unless Deland had blundered. She was a queer one—unfriendly with her own sex, which was bad. She said she disliked women. Then how in heaven's name did she think she could fill the job of superintendent of a hospital—even a small one like Rebecca Moore? He hadn't favored it from the first; but she was determined and look what happened! That was the worst of letting a woman in on one's plans. Now Doc added suspicion to his cool treatment of him. Roberta scorned him. He winced as he remembered her shrinking from his touch. She had even said she disliked him. Was it pique or had she really changed? Was the love she had declared for him quite dead? He wondered if Sylvia had made a confidante of Roberta the day she had called. He had tried his best to keep them apart. He felt no good could come from their meeting. Old Doc kept insisting Roberta would do Sylvia good—that Sylvia needed friends. He wished Doc would mind his own business. No doubt Sylvia was at the bottom of Roberta's changed manner. He found he really valued Roberta's esteem.

Doc had never wholly trusted him. He and his wife had nearly wrecked his wedding plans. Mrs. Holmes was one woman whose suspicions he was never able to dissipate. The old snob had spent years trying to influence Sylvia. But no one could swerve her. In fact, he felt sure the opposition served only to strengthen her determination to do as she pleased. He hadn't worried much. After all, Sylvia had complete control of her fortune and all their interference amounted to absolutely nothing. But he would never forget and in spite of Doc's sponsoring, there was little love lost between them.

Then, too, there was Chris, whom he hated. Chris, born to the purple, looked upon him as an interloper, a chiseler, a social climber. Deland had hinted at some sort of scandal in which both the flawless Chris and Roberta were mixed. He doubted it. Deland hated Roberta because she knew he found her attractive.

Jealous! Women were the very devil sometimes. He'd bet a dollar it was a woman who had thrown a wrench into the machinery of his smooth-running plans. He wished he knew who it was. Of course he had enemies. Long ago he had discovered most people with ambition had enemies.

He didn't hear the door open nor see Paula Winslow pause just inside the room. His fingers beat a nervous tattoo on the top of his polished desk. At last he got to his feet and strode to the long window overlooking the courtyard. He wished he had stayed in New York. Why had he ever come to this hick town anyway? Holmes hadn't any real authority over Sylvia. If he had put his foot down—had worked it right, Sylvia would have refused to listen to her uncle's insistence. But no, he thought he saw a chance to realize his ambition. Rebecca Moore was gaining quite a reputation. Holmes was his wife's uncle. What was more natural than for him to turn the hospital over to his promising nephew-in-law? It had looked absolutely fool-proof. He wished now he had tried to win over Lewis and Morrison who had no doubt been influenced by the Holmes' distrust of him. Later, when he was firmly entrenched, he could have edged them out. But Deland wanted Morrison's job. Somehow, he couldn't get away from the feeling that Deland was at the bottom of this debacle. Why had he listened to her? What did he care for her fool ambitions to become the superintendent of his hospital? As he saw it now, it never would have worked. An older Roberta in that job would be just about perfect; but of course that was out—now. Deland was altogether too possessive. She actually had the colossal nerve to threaten him. He could use his influence or else—— When it came right down to brass tacks, Rhoda hadn't a thing on him and he had told her so last night. She had been ugly and warned him not to be too sure. He was glad the Board had kicked her out. She was getting to be a nuisance. She should have known better than to come here last night. Suppose someone had seen her. There would be the devil to pay. He swore roundly and turned sharply as a light laugh startled him.

"Oh," he said, his face showing displeasure. "What's up? You know office hours are over. I'm just going out."

"Not until I have said what I came to say," Paula Winslow told him. "So, you've been kidding me all along. Now you intend casting me off for someone else who can be more useful to you. I saw her here last night with you. Don't take the trouble to deny it. Who was it? Some poor fool with something you want or who can feed your ego or use her influence to get you what you crave—power in this lousy town. I watched until she left and then saw you sneak out and go home to that poor simpleton who bought you—paid for your training so you'd marry her."

"Shut up!" he snapped. "You're drunk, Paula. I warned you to cut out alcohol."

"Shut up yourself," she retorted venomously. "I suppose you don't think I know it's your custom to lead women on until they lose their heads or cease to be of use to you, and then discard them. But this time you're going to pay for it, my handsome Casanova. I was idiot enough to think you meant it when you said you loved me; that your wife didn't understand your needs. I believed you when you talked of the South Seas and a Paradise alone with me. I know now you were using me—my influence with those senile old fools who control Rebecca Moore Board. You thought because of me they'd vote you in as assistant to Holmes. That they'd kick Morrison out and give her job to your 'favorite nurse.' You see, I know all about your little plans!

"Why, you—you poor deluded, conceited, fatuous dope, you haven't the brains of a mosquito or you'd know that bunch of fossils would never stand for your loose morals. I suppose you thought they didn't know how far you had gone—you've been so very careful to cover your tracks. You thought your good looks and perfect bedside manner could still put you over with every woman you met. You don't know this town, my dear doctor. Garsden still believes in the sanctity of marriage—in the purity of the home. I'm quite beyond the pale. Only family pride prevents my relatives from publicly disowning me. The very fact you've been going about with me is enough to damn you in Garsden's eyes. You didn't know that, did you, when you were so lavish with your attentions?" She laughed shrilly—crazily—and Stanley Nichols wished with all his soul Anna Hoxie would return.

"We're both in the same boat, Stan—tarred with the same pitch. You're absolutely done—finished, as far as Garsden's concerned. Even its god Holmes can't save you, and I intend putting the finishing touches. I could kill you quite simply, but that would be too easy on you. No, you will live and live and live and suffer. Don't look so scared, Doctor. I'm not going to hurt you—physically, although I would like to spoil your beauty—make you so repulsive women would recoil in horror when they saw you. Don't look at me like that. Do you hear!" Her voice rose hysterically.

"She's mad," Stan told himself with a shiver of something very like horror. Why didn't someone come —the telephone ring—anything to break the spell? With an effort, he forced a smile.

"Oh, come now, Paula," he soothed, his eyes holding hers. "You're drunk and imagining things. Sit down and I'll get you something to make you feel better. Just relax," his charming voice reached a seductive note. "Why, darling, you know how fond of you I am—we've been pals. What do either of us care for a lot of silly old busy-bodies? You and I have had a lot of fun. Now haven't we? You have been the only one in this hick town that mattered. You know that. Now be a good girl and sit down and forget you're mad. My office nurse will be back in a minute and you wouldn't want her to think you have been quarreling with me, would you?"

He had regained something of his old confidence. He had always been able to manage women no matter how screwy. His hand reached out to touch her, but she whirled away from him. She laughed again shrilly and her eyes blazed. She clutched a small revolver and he drew back.

"I'll show you," she cried and pointed the weapon, not at him but at her own heart. He sprang, involuntarily, toward her. They grappled for a moment. There was a shattering explosion. With a strangled cry, the doctor reeled, blood streaming from his mouth, then slowly sank to the floor.

Paula Winslow screamed horribly—eyes wide with terror. "Oh, Stan, darling—I didn't mean it—I didn't mean to hurt you. It was me—I'm—I'm sick of life——"

She picked up the fallen gun and pressed it to her breast. Footsteps raced along the corridor outside. A second deafening report coincided with the violent opening of the door. Paula Winslow's body lay across that of the young doctor.

Instantly the room was full of people. Anna Hoxie

fought her way through the crowd and knelt beside her employer.

"He isn't dead," she said. "Get a doctor. Call Holmes. Call the ambulance." She lifted Paula's body aside and stood up, her eyes menacing. "Get out of here, every one of you!"

It didn't require a very close examination to see that Paula Winslow was dead. Hoxie told herself she had been expecting something of the sort. Why did Doctor Nichols persist in taking such chances?

Two policemen entered without ceremony. "What's going on here?" one of them asked.

"You can see for yourself," Miss Hoxie replied crisply. Now that she knew the doctor was still alive, she had regained something of her natural poise. "Mrs. Winslow shot Doctor Nichols and then herself."

"Ye-ah?" one of the men muttered.

The door opened once more and Doctor Holmes strode into the room, his face white and haggard. He looked intently at the body of Paula, then briefly at Doctor Nichols.

"I suppose you can't keep this quiet?" he asked after a moment.

"Sorry, Doc. Can't be done," the officer addressed answered. "Murder and suicide, it looks like, don't it?"

"Doctor Nichols is not dead, officer," the old man replied. "The girl is. The shot pierced her heart. It is

[263]

not murder—merely suicide. It is quite evident she shot him and then herself."

The siren of the ambulance broke the sudden silence.

Back in Rebecca Moore, rumor was again rife. Something had happened. The ambulance had been sent to Doctor Nichols' swank office in the bank building. News of an accident to the doctor seeped through to 217 shortly after four o'clock when the ambulance returned with its burden. Miss Morrison called Roberta from Chris's room and suggested he be allowed to go to the Holmes residence at once instead of waiting until next day. Roberta was to accompany him. Doctor Nichols had met with an accident and the chief wanted Sylvia kept in complete ignorance until he should return home some time later. Would Roberta see that no visitors were admitted and no wild rumors reached her?

The Holmes limousine was waiting at the front entrance of the hospital when Roberta and Chris left his room a few minutes later.

"I wonder what it is," Roberta said worriedly, as the elevator lowered them to the first floor.

"And you are the girl who insisted nothing ever happened in this joint," jeered Chris. "I shouldn't wonder if one of Stan's indiscretions had at long last caught up with him."

"Don't," Roberta pleaded.

"Still carrying a torch for him, Robin?" he asked, his eyes searching her troubled face.

"No. I have not the slightest personal interest in Doctor Nichols, Chris," the girl said simply.

"Then why the tragic demeanor?"

"If anything happened to him it might kill his wife," she answered. "Sylvia adores her husband and you know her heart is not at all strong."

"I know it," Chris said. "The poor kid's given him everything and how does he repay her? By making love to every woman he meets."

"The hospital doesn't want a scandal——"

"Then you have an idea there is room for scandal?"

"Don't," she said again. "Let's not imagine things. Let's wait until we know the facts."

Was it Deland? Had she tried to injure Stan because of the failure of their plans? Or was it someone else? And just how badly was he hurt?

"Okay. You're the nurse," Chris agreed amiably.

Miss Morrison was in the main corridor when they left the elevator and walked beside Chris to the front door. Her face was grave and Roberta wished she might question her; but one didn't take liberties with the superintendent in spite of her friendliness and leniency.

"Good-bye, Morry," Chris said as they reached the door. He managed to shake hands although he still had difficulty with his crutches.

"It's not good-bye, Chris," she said. "You must drop in often—every day. It has been good seeing you again."

"I'll be seeing you," he promised, as he made his careful way down the two shallow steps and along the walk to the car. "I bet Sylvia will be surprised to see me today. What shall we tell her? That they kicked me out over there? You know that's what they used to do when I was a kid and made a nuisance of myself. I guess I had the idea the hospital was as much home as Uncle Doc's house."

"Tell her anything you like except the truth," Roberta advised him. "But how explain my presence with you? You don't need a nurse any more."

"Indeed I do—one nurse, Robin. Why can't I tell her about us—that we have decided to be married over again?"

"Over again? Still harping on that crazy stunt of two years ago? I'm afraid you have a one-track mind, Mr. Baxter. Don't be foolish, Chris."

"You may be surprised to hear that several people know about that same crazy stunt only they don't call it that," the young man said, seriously.

"What do you mean?" Roberta was startled.

"I didn't tell you because I didn't want to upset you. It seems Bert shot off his mouth to Marge in front of Deland that time he ran into you. He told her you had divorced me. I can see him crowing like a rooster over it. Deland wasn't particularly interested—or it didn't make much of an impression on her until I landed in the place, and you were assigned me as night nurse. Then it seems the lady began digging around. She found out that you had met Stan before he was married and she got it into her head there was something more than a mere doctor and nurse relationship between you."

"How terrible!" Roberta whispered, her face flaming.

"Terrible is right," Chris muttered, and went on. "She thought Stan was the other man in the case—that you had divorced me because of him. And being an opportunist she wangled the job of days on my case in order to gather the facts so she could get you kicked out. Because, my innocent darling, she thought you had the inside track with the handsome Stanley. Well, I told her plenty. I told her she was all wet as regarded your infatuation for my cousin's husband and that if she started anything I would personally see to it she was removed at once. I let her understand my influence was enormous and far-reaching, not only with my uncle but with the trustees as well. I let her think I had every hope the misunderstanding between you and me would be straightened out and we would live happily ever after. But even while I let off all that steam, Robin, I was scared stiff for fear I was mistaken—that you did love Stan although I felt sure you would never hurt Sylvia. Like all men in love, I was sure Stan loved you, too. That he married Sylvia for her money as the family had always surmised. It wasn't until I saw the same thing you did in the solarium one morning that I knew positively there was nothing that really mattered between you. You simply couldn't love a man of that type. I knew then what I had only imagined before, that Deland's insinuations were merely a smoke screen for her own protection. After that I went to work in earnest. I forgot my foot and concentrated on solving the mystery. I solved it—to date. Now, if what I fear is true, there will be another mystery to delve into."

"You are better, Chris," Roberta told him. "When you begin sleuthing, I know you are distinctly on the mend. Do you think she told anyone else—about—us?"

"No. I don't think she did. Rebecca Moore is opposed to married nurses. I'm not sure about divorcées, or widows. They would have had you on the carpet if they had suspected anything."

"But why has she kept silent? She always appeared to dislike me. I can't imagine why. I never harmed her in any way," Roberta said.

"Except by being beautiful and good," Chris replied. "Well, I put the fear of God in her. She believed I had all sorts of influence here, which is utter nonsense; but she didn't know that. Of course most of the trustees have known me since I was a youngster and lived here with Uncle Doc. They look upon me as a sort of ward. Anyway, they send me cards at Christmas and on birthdays and I always make the rounds when I'm home. Most of them are getting on in years but they are the backbone of this community. One or two have died but the jobs have been kept pretty much in the same families. No one kicks and everyone is happy."

"It's queer, Chris, but everything that has happened has occurred since Deland came."

Chris shook his head. "No. You'll find it antedates that by weeks, four anyway, Robin."

Roberta knew he meant the coming of Stan. They were approaching the Holmes mansion and Chris turned to the girl beside him.

"You haven't answered the question I asked some minutes back, Robin. Will you marry me—again? You know I love you and I'll move heaven and earth to make you happy."

Roberta sat silent for a long moment until the car pulled up at the front entrance and the chauffeur opened the door.

"Take it easy," she cautioned. "Better come with us," she advised the chauffeur. "I don't know about the steps."

"Yes, ma'am," the man said and followed closely.

But Chris managed the broad shallow stone steps very well and grinned as he rang the bell. "How about it, Robin?"

[269]

Robin searched in her purse for a moment then handed him a small plain gold wedding ring. His face paled and his eyes looked stricken as he lifted them to hers. He made no move to take it from her extended hand.

"But you'll need it, Chris," Roberta persisted, softly. "Isn't the groom supposed to slip it on his bride's finger? You didn't, you know—just ordered: 'Put this on.' Remember? Oh, darling, be careful!" she cried.

A crutch clattered to the floor as he reached for her. The door had opened and a startled butler surveyed the shocking spectacle of his master's nephew kissing a uniformed nurse on the front porch for all the world to see.

Chapter 22

THE SUICIDE OF PAULA WINSLOW PROVIDED A SOMEWHAT longer than the usual nine days' scandal, due, no doubt, to the prominence of the principals. But, after all, little blame was attached to Doctor Nichols. People knew he had many women patients and the fact he was handsome was surely no fault of his. Neither could he prevent women from making fools of themselves.

As for Paula Winslow—she had always been a problem—spoiled from infancy. Her parents had never been able to control her. She had been expelled from two fashionable boarding schools for wild escapades and the nice boy she married and almost ruined was considered well rid of her. So it was the woman who bore the brunt of the gossip and being dead she could do nothing to refute it.

The simple statement the young man wrote when he was able to do so, threatened to make him a hero. He told of attempting to prevent Mrs. Winslow from taking her own life. In the struggle the gun exploded, the bullet shattering his jaw. His patients wept for his lost beauty, for while plastic surgery could do much for him, his extraordinary good looks were gone together with his fascinating and flattering manner of talking. Hereafter his speech would be blurred—faltering. What was infinitely worse for a man in his profession, his confidence appeared to have completely vanished. So Paula Winslow had her revenge even though she wasn't above ground to enjoy it. Doctor Stanley Nichols had ceased to be a menace to female hearts.

On the day Roberta answered his request to come to the hospital to see him, Chris graduated to two canes. He saw no reason why Roberta should be at Stan's command. There were other nurses. How about Araminta, the infallible? Stan had gotten himself into this fix and he was darned lucky to escape with his life. But in spite of his dislike of the man, Chris knew a real pity for him because of the loss he had sustained. A loss that he knew meant much to him. He wondered if he would be able to rebuild his life from the ruins his folly had brought about. Perhaps with Sylvia's help he could. Uncle Doc said he had real ability. Maybe Uncle Doc was right. He hoped so for Sylvia's sake.

Roberta read shame and regret in Stanley Nichols' eyes and he clung to her hand as if seeking strength and reassurance from her. A feeling of compassion swept all the bitterness and hurt from her heart.

"It's all right, Stan," she said softly. "I know. Let us forget what is past and look only to the future."

He wrote for a moment and Roberta read:

"Uncle Doc told me about you and Chris. Good luck, Berta!"

"I'm very happy, Stan," she said simply. "I think I loved him from the first. Sylvia wants you to come home. And now that Chris is better, she has asked me to take care of you until you are quite well again."

He pressed her hand and his eyes thanked her.

"She is so sweet, Stan, and she loves you with all her heart." His eyes filled with tears and to lighten the sadness, Roberta smiled and asked teasingly:

"How about that theory of yours, Stan, that a man will co-operate better with a strange nurse than with one he knows? Maybe we'd better send——"

He wrote hastily: "Please, Berta! Do you mind?"

"Of course not. Between us, Sylvia and I will have you up and about again before you know it."

During the weeks of his convalescence, Stanley Nichols' entire nature underwent a change. Gone was the old trifling—the conceit—the almost lordly manner in which he demanded admiration and accepted it as his due. He wanted his wife with him constantly and Sylvia glowed with love and pride in him, seeming to gain strength from his very weakness and need of her. One day she slipped her hand into Roberta's and whispered tensely:

[273]

"Oh, Roberta, I'm glad it happened! Am I wicked to say that? If so, I'm wicked, for it's the way I feel. There have been times when I felt he didn't really belong to me—that I had only the shell—not even that—merely the shadow. I never told anyone, but I was terribly jealous. I knew women admired him—he was so charming—so amazingly good-looking! Now, I feel I have the real Stanley—the Stan who worked desperately hard to get an education—to fit himself, he used to say, for a place beside me."

She laughed softly.

"He insisted he broke Jacob's record to bits, because he served three times seven years for me. Isn't it beautiful to be loved so much? You understand, because Chris loves you although he didn't have to serve for you as Stan did for me. And to think I hesitated to accept his love. I thought he ought to marry an active, healthy girl who could give him strong sons and daughters; but he made me see that I was all he had ever wanted. We could adopt children if we wanted them, but I was the only wife he could ever have. I used to be afraid, sometimes, but I shall never be again, for now I am sure—so blessedly sure!"

Roberta laid her cheek upon the thin one pressed against her shoulder. Once she had almost hated this frail, lovely girl for coming between her and the man she loved. Now, she knew it was not love, but infatuation she had felt for Stanley Nichols—infatuation for his smooth line and good looks. She thought contentedly of Chris with his complete and wholesome sincerity; his rugged manliness and charm so infinitely more desirable than mere physical beauty. Her heart sang with happiness.

May merged into June. With Stan well on the way to recovery, Roberta yielded to her sister's pleading to bring Chris to Shandleys Beach. The weather was glorious and Will and Prunella wanted to pass upon the man she had decided to marry.

Doctor Holmes insisted that his chauffeur, Dan, drive them in the big car; but Chris held out for Jeremiah. He had never ridden in the old wreck and confessed to a deep affection for it. Hadn't it brought him Robin?

So it was that on one of those perfect days—rare even in June—they set out for Shandleys Beach. Chris, now managing very well with one cane, settled himself beside Roberta with all the eagerness of a small boy facing some thrilling adventure. Jeremiah was on his best behavior.

"We'll take the short cut at Faber Corners, Chris," Roberta announced as they neared the road turning east. "It will take us past the Palmers' and, if you want to, we can stop for a moment."

"Okay. I'd like to see the place of our first brief honeymoon."

Roberta laughed. "I assure you it wasn't at all my idea of a honeymoon, darling."

"It wasn't so bad—only for the interruptions. If Bert and his wife hadn't barged in on us we could have enjoyed that swell meal you prepared and—maybe you wouldn't have heard the plow go past." He touched her cheek gently, then chuckled at his own sentiment.

"Oh, yes, I should. My hearing is excellent."

They reached the Palmer cottage only to find it closely shuttered—deserted. The grass had not been cut nor the yard cleared of its accumulation of winter debris.

"I have an idea, Robin," Chris said enthusiastically. "Let's rent the place for a second honeymoon. I'll get hold of Meta through the bank and see if she will let us have it for a month. We'll be near your people—not too near—but I'll get to know them before I carry you west. How about it?"

"Not so fast," Roberta cried. "We're not married yet."

"But soon, Robin. Next week at latest. I've waited two whole years—surely you won't keep me dangling any longer. Long engagements are things I heartily dislike."

"Long engagement, indeed! We have been engaged just exactly three weeks and four days, Chris Baxter," Roberta said.

"So what?" he asked. "Give me seven good reasons

have her loosen her hold of the visitor's hair to clutch a handful of her father's.

So, linked together by the small hands of the baby, the two men followed the others to the house. Prunella had vanished but from the kitchen beyond came a low mournful plaint to the accompaniment of spoon beating briskly against bowl as the old negress resumed her interrupted preparations for dinner.

Quite unconsciously, Roberta gave a sigh of relief. Prunella approved.

THE END